PENGUIN BOOKS

ONE PART WOMAN

PERUMAL MURUGAN is the star of contemporary Tamil literature, having garnered both critical acclaim and commercial success for his work. An award-winning writer, poet and scholar, he has written several novels, short-story collections, poetry anthologies and works of non-fiction. Some of his novels have been translated into English to immense acclaim, including *Seasons of the Palm*, which was shortlisted for the Kiriyama Award in 2005, and *One Part Woman*, his best-known work, which was shortlisted for the Crossword Award and won the prestigious ILF Samanvay Bhasha Samman in 2015. Murugan has also received awards from the Tamil Nadu government as well as from Katha Books.

ANIRUDDHAN VASUDEVAN is a performer, writer and translator. He documents various public health projects and art projects, and is involved in LGBT advocacy work. He is currently a PhD student in anthropology at the University of Texas, Austin, and is also working on his first novel.

ONE PART WOMAN

PERUMAL MURUGAN

Translated from the Tamil by
ANIRUDDHAN VASUDEVAN

PENGUIN BOOKS

PENGUIN BOOKS

Published by the Penguin Group

Penguin Books India Pvt. Ltd, 7th Floor, Infinity Tower C, DLF Cyber City, Gurgaon 122002, Haryana, India

Penguin Group (USA) Inc., 375 Hudson Street, New York, New York 10014, USA

Penguin Group (Canada), 90 Eglinton Avenue East, Suite 700, Toronto, Ontario, M4P 2Y3, Canada

Penguin Books Ltd, 80 Strand, London WC2R 0RL, England

Penguin Ireland, 25 St Stephen's Green, Dublin 2, Ireland (a division of Penguin Books Ltd)

Penguin Group (Australia), 707 Collins Street, Melbourne, Victoria 3008, Australia

Penguin Group (NZ), 67 Apollo Drive, Rosedale, Auckland 0632, New Zealand

Penguin Books (South Africa) (Pty) Ltd, Block D, Rosebank Office Park, 181 Jan Smuts Avenue, Parktown North, Johannesburg 2193, South Africa

Penguin Books Ltd, Registered Offices: 80 Strand, London WC2R 0RL, England

First published in Tamil as *Maadhorubaagan* by Kalachuvadu Publications, Tamil Nadu 2010
First published in English in Hamish Hamilton by Penguin Books India 2013
Published in Penguin Books 2014

Copyright © Perumal Murugan 2010
Translation copyright © Aniruddhan Vasudevan 2013

ISBN 9780143423546

Typeset in Bembo Std by Eleven Arts, Keshav Puram, New Delhi
Printed at Replika Press Pvt. Ltd, India

A PENGUIN RANDOM HOUSE COMPANY

ONE PART WOMAN

one

The portia tree was dense with foliage. If you looked closely, you could see the yellow trumpet-like flowers with their flared mouths, and the drooping, fading red ones with their inviting smiles. Portia flowers always grow more beautiful as they fade. Kali leapt up and plucked one. He never could resist the desire to possess what attracted him. The leaves came ripped, but the flower was intact. Settling down on the cot, he smelled the flower. It had a mild fragrance, that too when held close to the nose. He felt he should have left it on the tree. The sight of the flower on the tree was more beautiful than its scent.

He ran his eyes over the tree. It was he who had planted it there, in the front yard of his father-in-law's home. Before that, whenever he had visited this house, the sight of the bare front yard had hurt his eyes relentlessly. This forced him to remain indoors until the sun went down, and because of his presence, the womenfolk could not carry on their private chatter. So he spoke to his brother-in-law about it.

'Wouldn't it be good to have a tree here?'

1

'They refuse to have one. They say they need the sun to dry groundnuts and corn. Why don't you try talking to my father?'

Kali didn't do anything at the time. However, on his next visit, he brought along a stalk. On the way, he only smiled when Ponnayi said, 'Why are you lugging this along, maama?' She gave him an affectionate punch on his cheek and said, 'You hardly say anything. All I get is that bewitching smile!'

It had been just three months into their marriage, and they refused to stay away from each other even for a little while. They couldn't even resist constantly looking at each other's faces. But that day, when he visited his father-in-law's place, he didn't enter the house. He grabbed a rake and a spade and got started on his work immediately. He found a place to plant the stalk, a spot where it could grow without hindrances and be able to spread its branches in all directions. Even when it was just a stalk, Kali's mind could see the tree it would grow into one day. He could see how it would look ten, twenty years later.

He had got this stalk from the portia tree in his cattle enclosure back home. No one knew when that other tree had been planted. The gigantic spread of that tree was etched in his mind, and he hoped this one too would grow the same way. He imagined how the front yard would look when the tree spread its branches over it. Even while planting it, he focused on the pleasure of being able to lie in its cool shade some day. No one objected to the new son-in-law's fancies.

2

Even before the cow-dung bandage at the end of the stalk dried, shoots started sprouting. There was now an obligation to protect the tree that the son-in-law had planted. Afraid that she would forget to water the tree amidst all her chores, his mother-in-law started washing dishes right under the tree. She also kept a big pot of water there for people to wash their hands and feet when they came back from somewhere. So the space under the tree was always wet. And whenever Kali visited, that was the first spot he went to, making note of the tree's growth.

'Your son-in-law comes here only to make sure we're taking good care of his dowry!'

His father-in-law's teasing became a regular feature. The tree was called 'the son-in-law's dowry'. Just as he was never called by his name, neither was his tree. In just one year, it grew so tall that one could stand to full height under the new branches. After all, it had come from another tree that had withstood the vagaries of time. The next year, there were flowers. And then fruits.

Twelve years went by in a flash; the tree kept growing and spreading every year. Now ten cots could lie in its shade. It didn't shed much, but when it did, his mother-in-law would complain, 'This is an endless task—this sweeping, cleaning and taking care of my son-in-law's dowry!' His father-in-law delighted at the sight of the compost pits getting filled with the tree's leaves. The tree gave as much manure as a cow did, and it was definitely enough for one enclosure. What the son-in-law had given them was certainly a gift!

In the past two years or so, when Kali did not visit, the arms of the tree stretched towards the sky. Only when a tree is small can you notice its growth. When it is bigger, it continues to grow, but imperceptibly. Kali, however, could always size up a tree. For instance, he could now see that they had trimmed a branch that had outgrown the yard and started reaching into the house. It looked like a deformed body part. They must have done it to get some sun to dry something. But he stood looking at the tree's wound for a while.

Since he had not visited for two years, Ponnayi had not either. But this year, her brother, Muthu, had especially come to invite them. He arrived on the very first day of the festival in Karattur, the day when the flag was hoisted and the festivities began. He was adamant that they should come this year. Kali could not refuse. So he sent Ponnayi on the day the chariot was taken out in procession. But his plan was to go on the last day—the day the deities went back to the hill—so that he could stay one more day, feast on the meat and return home with Ponnayi. After all, how long could he lie under the tree and stare at its canopy, even though he was the one to have planted it?

His brother-in-law, Muthu, was his friend from childhood. In fact, they were so close that at some point he felt comfortable enough to freely say, 'I want to marry your sister.' But they had drifted apart once they became brothers-in-law. The gulf between them seemed to have become permanent over the years, but nothing much could be done about it. If he stayed here and worked the fields, people would openly ridicule him. They would say, 'See! He is his father-in-law's slave!' Also, he'd have to abandon everything back home to come here. His mother might be able to take care of the cow, the calves and the goats for a few days. But after that, she'd definitely start hurling abuses at him.

'Does he think the cows here would somehow feed themselves if he sits on his haunches in his father-in-law's house and eats away? Shouldn't a farmer be concerned about these poor creatures? It is only as long as this Marayi is alive that you can drop everything and run off like this. I could die any day. What would you do then?'

He knew when her tirade of abuses was likely to begin. If he delayed even a day or two, angry words were sure to pour forth from her rotten mouth. His father's face would appear before his eyes, like a mirage in the afternoon sun. That was all he recollected of his father. It was his mother who had raised him. And she made sure no one had the chance to say that a child raised by a widow would amount to nothing. She was adamant that they be treated equal to everyone else. She knew everything from ploughing the land to drawing water for the fields. 'We should not depend on anyone,' she would say.

One year, she could not find anyone to sow seeds. They said, 'Nothing would grow when sown by a woman in white,' clearly referring to her widow's attire. She tried calling a few people, but to no avail. Then she said, 'Let whatever grows grow. Or maybe nothing will. Then that's fine too. I don't care.' And she sowed the seeds herself. Nothing untoward happened; her yield was as good as anyone else's.

The day Kali grew strong enough to carry the basket, she handed it to him. She was there to help him until he learned the skill of sowing evenly, but after that it became his responsibility. However, wherever he roamed, Kali was under his mother's control. Before his marriage, he was a free spirit. It was hard to get hold of him on days when there was no work. If someone asked Marayi, she said, 'Where can that dog go? It must have dug up a spot in the shade somewhere and must be lying in it. Or else, it must be roaming around, getting tired. Wherever it is, it will come back at night to eat.' He never betrayed her trust, and he gave his best in the field. Even now, he would tend to his field and keep to himself. Having moved away from the minions of his youth, he would not go anywhere to idle around with anyone. This fenced enclosure was his lot. That's just the way things were.

two

He lay on the cot and closed his eyes. When the body realizes there is no work to do, it throws open its doors to weariness. Ponna was happy that Kali had come as promised. Even from where Kali was lying, he could sense her prancing around the house as though she had just been married. Wherever in the house she might be, he always knew what she'd be up to. She pervaded his thoughts. She came to occupy them so much that he could tell her every movement and gesture. His nostrils could now sense that she was making snacks for him. He even knew what snack it would be.

She woke him up a little while later. 'Maama, maama,' she called to him affectionately. She was holding a plate of snacks in her hands—hot pakodas and kacchayam, made with rice. He roused himself as if from a deep sleep. A smile lit up her entire face, spreading to her eyes, nose, cheeks and forehead. Kali wondered how Ponna managed to make every part of her face smile. Keeping the plate on his lap, Ponna sat down on the floor.

'Did you see the tree?' he asked. The pakoda melted with a crunch in his mouth.

'Yes, I see it every time I come here,' she said uninterestedly.

'No, dear one. Look up. See how it has grown. You can't even begin to count the flowers and the top-shaped fruits!' he said excitedly.

'Ponna, come here!' her mother yelled from inside the house. 'Shred this jaggery for me.'

'Coming!' she yelled. Turning back to Kali, she said, 'This was planted when we got married. Twelve years have gone by.' She sighed.

A shadow fell on her face. She must have been thinking about how the tree had grown so lush and abundant in twelve years while not even a worm had crawled in her womb. Every wretched thing reminded her of that lack.

After the wedding, she had fought with her father and had taken a cow from here. It delivered seven or eight calves, populating Kali's barn with its offspring. She'd tear up just looking at that cow. She had once cried out loud, 'I don't have the boon that even this mute creature has been blessed with.' Her tears filled him with rage against that cow and its calves. He felt like killing them all. But when he looked at their faces, he would melt: 'Poor things. What can they do about our suffering?'

'Palm jaggery adds a special taste to the kacchayam,' he said, trying to change the subject. He tore a piece and held it to her lips.

'Yes! Now is when your love pours forth,' she said

in mock anger and proceeded to take the morsel into her mouth.

Her mother called from inside: 'Come here, girl. The oil's heating up.'

'She can't stand it even for a little while! Nallayi is devious. It's not for no reason that they say she knows no time or place. Why is she yelling so much now?' Ponna got up and went in.

His eyes were fixed on her as she walked away. Her body had stayed firm. As he gazed after her, desire welled up within him, and he wanted her right then. But they had no privacy here, at his in-laws' home. When they were just married, space was made for them by rearranging sacks of harvested kambu millets and pulses. But when he was no longer a new son-in-law, he got a cot in the porch or in front of the house. He was itching to drag her and take her home.

The midday sun tormented his body. During the monsoons, he stayed home cuddling with her. It had occurred to him a few times that had she borne a child perhaps she too would have become haggard like the other women. When thoughts of women first came to him, it was Ponna's body that teased and tortured him incessantly. Unable to bear the agony, he tried to avoid looking at her. But his mind's eye would somehow seek her out. That had not changed to this day. But, whenever he embraced her, succumbing to the tease, it occurred to him that it was not the same embrace as before. Earlier, there was an urgency and passion to get to know her anew each time. That had dried up now. Now even when he took his face close to hers, his mind started worrying, 'Will it happen at least this time?' That was enough to put out the fire, and only ashes bloomed in the embers of his passion. In an attempt to douse it all with water, he started going about it mechanically. 'God, please bless us this time. Make it happen somehow,' he kept repeating. It all went up in smoke.

For seven or eight years now, there had been talk of a second marriage—both openly and secretively. As a result, many people had become the objects of Ponnayi's hatred. Chellappan, who dealt in cattle, came to the barnyard once. One of Kali's cows had failed to yield a calf despite two or three attempts at mating her with a bull. He'd wanted to get rid of the cow by selling it to Chellappan. While they were talking, Ponna was cleaning the floor, ridding it of cow dung. She never stayed put when she came to the barnyard. Even if Kali had just removed the dung, she would clean the floor of the cattle shed right away. She would give the calves a bath and tether them elsewhere; then she'd feed them. Mostly, it was she who cleaned out the goat refuse. She was focused on her work while Kali was talking to Chellappan. But Chellappan kept his gaze fixed on her as he tied up his hair in a knot. 'It is fate, mapillai,' said Chellappan, using the colloquial variation of 'maapillai' or 'son-in-law', also a term of friendly address between two men. 'That is just how some cows are. No matter what you do, they never get pregnant. Just quietly change the cow. If you say yes, I can fetch you one right away.'

He said it with a smile, but Ponna immediately understood the sense behind it. She felt as though a huge rock had been pressed against her heart. She wanted to drag him by the hair and thrash him with a whip. Instead, she picked up the stick that was lying in a corner of the cowshed and hit the cow on its legs and back. The poor creature. With panic in its eyes, it ran around the shed trying to dodge this unexpected attack.

'It has no sense of time and place. Shouldn't it know I was picking up the dung? It keeps stepping on my foot. It's come just to incur my wrath. Are you trying to get smart with me? I will cut off your tail, you wretched creature!'

Chellappan ran away saying, 'All right, mapillai! I will see you later.'

He never came back. But when Kali met him elsewhere, he said, 'That is how some cows are. If you go in front of them, they attack you with their horns. If you go behind them, they kick you. Your plight is difficult.' Sometimes he would say, 'Mapillai! Shall I find a new cow for you?'

Kali would reply, 'Come to the barnyard, uncle. We will discuss the matter.'

'Oh no! You think you can fuel the fire and watch the riot? Your cow is your business. Leave me alone!' And Chellappan would drop the subject.

Even though Kali was trying to be funny, these conversations made him extremely sad. He lamented the fact that he had become the butt of ridicule in the village.

Ponna never tired from lashing out at anyone who came to the barnyard talking about this. She did everything short of thrashing them with the broomstick. So no one brought it up when she was around. But they never failed to do so when they caught him alone.

three

During moments of intimacy, Ponna would ask, 'Maama, are you planning to abandon me and marry another woman? Tell me.'

He would cajole her. 'You are the apple of my eye—my pearl, my treasure. How can I ever leave you?'

'That's what I like to hear.' Saying this, she would melt.

But he also felt like teasing her. 'I will never abandon you. Even if another woman comes, I won't abandon you.'

'Chee!' she would push him away and cry. This was no joking matter for her.

When she saw people come and go, she would ask, 'Was this about a marriage alliance?'

'Hmm,' he would nod.

'Has it been fixed?'

'Almost.'

'What will be my plight then?'

'You can stay in a corner,' he would say.

She would cry herself to exhaustion. 'Is it my fate that

I should beg for food from another woman? I will leave right away for my father's house. They will feed me at least once a day, wouldn't they? After all, they gave birth to me. Don't I have a brother? I will fall at his feet. Won't he feed me porridge for the rest of my life? If nothing works, can't I find a small rope? Doesn't the portia tree have its branches spread all over? I will hang from one of those.'

Watching her antics, Kali would secretly smile to himself. Ponna would behave as if everything was over and he had already brought another woman home. He wondered if she was rehearsing for such a moment. It always took days to placate her.

This was their game. If they'd had children playing around the house, they wouldn't have needed this. Such games were just a ploy to keep themselves from getting bored looking at each other's faces. But he had no thought of marrying another girl.

'One torture is enough for this birth,' he would say.

'Oh! You think I am torturing you?' And she would get furious. But when she said, 'Maama, won't I ever get pregnant?' his heart would melt and he would rush to comfort her.

'Why not, dear? You are only twenty-eight now. You were sixteen when I married you. And you look just the same. Women are giving birth right till they are forty and forty-five. We are not that old.' Their hearts swung between faith and resignation.

Neither of them had had their birth charts made. If he asked his mother about the time of his birth, she would lament, 'I struggled for two days after my water broke. Who took care of me? The midwife somehow saved both our lives. I prayed to Badrakali. That's why I named you Kaliyannan. I don't even remember if it was the month of Maasi or Panguni. Do you think we are royalty to have the time and day of birth noted down? What's the use of a birth chart for someone who rolls in the dust? Even if you rub yourself with oil before rolling, you will have to be content with whatever sticks to you.'

Ponna, too, did not have the details of her birth written down. So they both showed their hands to palmists everywhere and had to be content with what they were told. Whenever she went to the market, Ponna would go to have her card read by a parrot. She had been to every astrologer in the area who picked cards using a parrot. They all predicted good tidings. Not even once was a bad card drawn. During fairs, there were even those who made predictions by drawing lines. Some used large pearls, others had pebbles piled up. It didn't cost too much—perhaps one or two rupees. All of them predicted good things. If she mentioned that she'd been married for over ten years, they would say, 'You will get it late, but you will get it for sure.'

In hard times, all threads of faith would come together.

four

Kali was wiping his hands after finishing the hot pakodas and sweetened rice cakes when Ponna brought another plate of snacks and a mug of water. Whenever they came here for a feast, they claimed this space under the tree. Night or day, this was where they stayed. The house was a secluded one in the middle of the fields, so there were no intrusions. If it started drizzling, he moved to the porch. But he never went inside the house, which was comprised only of one big room. Apart from Muthu, his wife and child, this space was also shared by Kali's father-in-law and mother-in-law. His father-in-law, too, would keep to the porch and the cattle enclosure. Even Muthu would only enter the house at night to sleep.

'Have you taken the blessing money for the festival?' Kali asked Ponna.

'Like that's the only thing lacking in my life. If I had one child each in my arms, on my waist and in my womb, I would demand it rightfully from my father and brother.

Now, if they give it to me, I will take it. If they don't, I will not ask.'

They hadn't been to the temple chariot festival for two years. Before that, it used to be an elaborate affair with a new sari, dhoti, towel, and so on. They were even gifted up to ten or twenty rupees as money to offer to the gods. It was not that Kali had come to expect any of this as a matter of routine. But he was only trying to make conversation and wanted to know her thoughts.

Holding her hand affectionately, Kali made her sit on the cot. The cloth covering her bosom slipped slightly as she sat down. Kali's eyes penetrated the fabric. Quickly pulling it back in place, she said, 'Look where your eyes stray in the middle of the day!'

He replied, taking mock offence, 'If I can't see them, then what are they for?'

'Hey, Ponna!' came her mother's yell, 'Come here now and attend to the lentils. How many things can I handle at once?'

'The old hag is not able to do anything on her own,' Ponna said as she got up. Seeing the brightness on his face, she laughed, reached for the knot in his hair and undid it before running into the house.

She had great fondness for the little knot of hair on his head. She often untied it and played with his locks, often by braiding them. 'Your hair is thicker than mine, maama,' she'd say. 'But there is no little petal of a hand that could hold this and climb up your shoulders.'

She managed to connect anything to the subject of children. It was not a worry she could keep hidden within herself. Even if she did, people would come to know anyway. She had no other thought besides trying to pre-empt other people's questions about this.

Last year, avoiding the fast, Kali took Ponna to see the chariot festival. It was the day the big chariot was taken around. People from the villages nearby were swarming the streets. When you are in a crowd, your spirits are somehow lifted. When they were surveying the shops, he heard someone call out, 'Hey, Kali, are you well?'

Bommidi Mani was smiling from the other side of the crowd. It had been several years since he left the village. He had settled down on his own land in Bommidi. He shouted from where he stood, 'Do you have children?' Kali went pale. Even though the crowd carried on as before, he felt as if everyone had turned to look at him. Thankfully, Ponna was inside the bangle shop.

Embarrassed, he gestured a no. Mani smacked himself on the head to express his sympathy with Kali's fate and said, 'Get married again.' Kali had to smile it away and vanish into the crowd. It annoyed Kali that though they might have a million things wrong with their own lives, people found great pleasure in poking and prodding other people's miseries. Couldn't they even remember they were in a public place? What kind of pride comes from knowing that the other person does not have what one has? Does everyone have everything? Isn't there always something lacking?

Someone or the other always appeared to remind him of it. 'I may or may not have children. What is it to you? Shut up and leave!' he felt like yelling. But he never could. What stopped him from reciprocating their rudeness? Ponna was able to give cheeky retorts. He could not.

His mother believed that going to Kaliyur to see the astrologer was the solution to every problem. The man would make his predictions only once a week when, after finishing his routine task of climbing palm trees, he would come to a little shrine under a tree in the forest. This would be at around ten in the morning. The ritual was simple. It was important to cut open a lemon—this signified a sacrifice. He would then divide a cluster of beads into two sets, taking the bunch on the right-hand side in both his hands and shaking them. He would then proceed to arrange them in pairs. If a single bead remained, things would be in one's favour. But if they all paired up, it was cause for worry. Every time Kali and Ponna had been to him so far, they had always drawn a single, unpaired bead. So the astrologer believed that they would definitely be blessed with a child.

'There is some curse that you have inherited. Everything will be all right if we find out what that is and make offerings for appeasement,' he said once.

Kali's mother did not know what curse it was. 'Why should you suffer for what some dog might have done?' she cried. But something occurred to her after she thought about it for a few days. She remembered an incident. It was from the time of Kali's great-grandfather, Nachimuthu.

One year, the yield of castor seeds was high in his fields, and he would invariably carry a sack or two to the market every week. One particular week, he took two sacks and unloaded them under a tamarind tree. The merchant, who usually bought the castor seeds, was there as usual, sitting with his men and his measuring mugs. In those days, one padi of castor seeds fetched only an anna. It was great luck if a sack fetched you five rupees.

When Nachimuthu unloaded his sacks of castor seeds, a cart loaded with sacks arrived from Pazhaiyur. It was clearly from a bigger farm, but they had no one to unload the sacks.

The merchant said, 'Please help with unloading these. I'll get you paid for it.'

Nachimuthu did the task obligingly. But in the end the numbers did not tally. 'There were fourteen sacks,' said the driver of the cart. There were only thirteen on the ground.

And, curiously, the two sacks that Nachimuthu had brought as his own had now grown to three. The merchant noticed that and remarked, 'I thought you had only two.'

If Nachimuthu had said, 'I unloaded one here by mistake,' the issue might have ended there. Instead, he swore that he had brought three sacks. The driver of the cart from Pazhaiyur was not going to leave the matter there. So it went to the temple.

All unresolved issues went to the Karattur Murugan temple. Halfway up the hill, on the seventieth step, Murugan stands carved on the rock. There is even a belief that long ago this was the main temple on the hill. When the hill was covered with dense forest, the dwellers made this deity. This original god still made sure truth prevailed. Once the seventy steps of truth began, people bent down in obeisance on every step. Even though steps have been carved up to the top of the hill and another, bigger temple has sprouted there, this Murugan on the seventieth step is the original god.

Every step had a stone lamp. Whenever there was a matter to be settled in the temple, the plaintiff filled each lamp with oil and lit them. The defendant was made to snuff out each lamp and arrive at Murugan's feet and swear that he or she did not do what they had been accused of. Nachimuthu put out all seventy lamps. Thinking of Murugan as just an image scratched on a rock, he swore at his feet. For just a sack of castor seeds, for a meagre five rupees, he perjured in front of a god.

They say that soon after this incident, Nachimuthu lost his mind and wandered all over town. Apparently, he pulled everyone by the hand saying, 'Come, let's go to the Murugan on the seventieth step.' No one knew what happened to him once he left the village and started wandering the streets of Karattur. Kali's grandfather was his only child. His father, too, had been his grandfather's only child. They both died young. Amma narrated all this and started crying.

Seeking redemption from this curse, Kali and Ponna scaled the hill. For seventy days, they lit the seventy lamps and cast themselves at Murugan's feet, pleading for his blessings.

The entire castor seed yield from that year became the oil in those lamps. But even that was not enough. So they bought more, took some in alms, and continued to fill those lamps. They even tried pacifying Murugan's anger by smearing oil on the deity's body.

They would leave in their cart at dusk. By the time they would tether the bulls at the foot of the hill, having requested the flower vendor to keep an eye on them, and climb and reach the seventieth step, the day would have ended. The priest would be waiting for them. Kali filled the lamps with oil, and Ponna lighted them. The priest bathed Murugan every day in castor oil. The belief was that only castor oil could appease a century-long wrath. When they finished the rituals and climbed down the hill, the town would have gone to bed. But nothing could placate Murugan.

Kali's grandmother, however, had another explanation. She took umbrage at her daughter-in-law's story of the family curse. 'Was it your mother who came as the merchant who bought the castor seeds?' she said. 'Who knows which dog stole the sack? She is unloading that crime on my family. No one has ever told me this story. Your mother must have stayed up many nights to come up with it. What does she know? She can't even count! She came into the family so much later. But never mind. You lit the lamps for god. Only good can come out of it.'

But until the day she died, his grandmother was worried about the perpetuation of her lineage. She sent the young couple to any temple festival anywhere, saying, 'Go and beg for alms.' They did all of that, but nothing came of it.

Furthermore, Kali's grandmother had a different story to tell—one that competed with his mother's theory of their current predicament. He thought they were vying with each other to narrate stories of curses and retribution. He lamented his fate that he had to do anything they asked him to do. He feared that if he refused, Ponna would unleash her tirade. She would behave as if doing that one thing would finally ensure childbirth. Such was the case with his grandmother's story too. But this one, though full of words, did not travel far either.

five

In those times, the region around Karattur was covered with forests. It was the farmers who converted it gradually into cultivable land. In the beginning, while they were engaged in this daunting task, they would also take their herds of cattle to graze in this area. Young men went daringly into the forest for this reason. Once, four such daring youths went herding their goats. In the heat of midday, they heard a female voice screaming in agony from within the forest.

There were many ghost stories about the forest. At first they thought it was the snare of Mohini who was said to bewitch young men. But the voice sounded steady and human, so they walked in its direction, although fearfully. It was autumn, and the trees had all shed their leaves and were standing bare. Only the neem and palm trees were lush, with their foliage still intact. Then they saw her sitting under a palm tree, wearing only a chequered wrap around her waist. Her breasts had freshly blossomed. She was a forest dweller, fourteen or fifteen years of age.

The boys knew that tribal people lived in the forest. Once in a while, they ventured into the town in tens or fifteens to barter things in exchange for what they needed. They were not an agrarian community. They ate roots, shoots and fruits. Millets were the only grains they accepted from the fields.

The girl was from that community. Some adolescent anger had made her leave her haven and reach the edge of the forest. She was determined to stay there until her people came looking for her. At first, the four men looked at her with sympathy. But it dawned on them that the girl was all alone, and they were soon overcome with the urge of youth. Even though she was a girl made strong by life in the forest, she could not fight the hard-work-forged strength of the four young men. She could do nothing. Not only did they ravish her, they also strangled her to death and rolled her into a ditch in the forest. They might have thought that that would ensure their safety. But on the third day, an unidentifiable fragrance of a tree rose from the pit where she lay, and spread all around. Her people followed the scent and eventually found her dead body.

The four men fled the town fearing the arrows of the tribal people. No one knew what happened to them. Many stories flourished. Some said they hanged themselves. Some even said they went away to a distant country and were happily married. Time went by; the forest was gradually uprooted and turned into cultivable land.

Once, during a famine, when a few people went westward herding their cattle, they were surprised to see their family deity, Badrakali, enshrined there. When they asked around about it, they were told that the goddess had been brought there by ancestors who came from distant lands. No one knew the name of that faraway place—it seemed that the ancestors had failed to mention it. Some people presumed that the ancestors being spoken about were, in fact, the same four young men who had fled the place ages ago. The descendants of those four men would thus be long-lost relatives with whom these people now reconnected.

But it was also believed that the tribal girl's curse hounded even those families that dared to associate with them: 'Devatha, our goddess who resides up in that hill, will seek justice from those who did this to me. No girl child will ever be born in their families. Even the male children shall grow up to be impotent and die young.'

This curse of the tribal girl persisted till today. That was why no girl child had been born in this lineage. Even those that were born had died in a day or two. The men, too, had truncated lives.

Kali's grandmother narrated all this and launched into a dirge. She lamented the fact that she could not keep the family secret from him. But she tried to keep his faith alive: 'Dear one, you have a good heart. You will have four or five children, and you will live to be a hundred.'

Kali wondered if he too would die young. But a little faith grew in his heart, that a child might actually be born, even if he would grow up to be impotent. Was childbirth getting delayed to postpone his early death? A child could be born even when he was forty. And he might live to see it for eight or ten years. That was what had happened to his father and grandfather.

He did not remember his father's face clearly. But there was one image that was etched in his mind, thanks to his mother's periodic narration of it. His father had always suffered from severe abdominal pain. Toddy and arrack were his staple food. 'My Kalimma' was how he used to lovingly address Kali, and he took Kali on his shoulders wherever he went. It is likely that the way he addressed Kali expressed his sadness at not having a girl child. So Kali wondered if he too would have a male child and live to be fifty years or so. Wasn't that enough?

As if she read his thoughts, Ponna ruffled his hair and pulled him close to her breast. When she heard what his grandmother had to share, she lamented her fate at having to marry into a family with so many curses weighing it down. But Kali's suffering made her forget her own. She feared she might have to part with him soon. Other than the lack of a child they could call their own, there was nothing else missing in their lives. He fulfilled every wish of hers, perhaps because he had married her out of love.

The day he found out that his mother and his wife did not get along, he asked his mother to cook her own food. She made a scene, crying, 'I gave birth to just one son, and I struggled so much to bring you up.'

He said, 'I have not gone away anywhere. I am right here next door. And I take care of you in all other ways. What's the point in staying together when you two cannot get along? This might improve your relationship.' And it happened just like he said. In fact, sometimes the two women even got together and turned on Kali, making it doubly hard for him. Now that they had been told the story of the tribal girl and her curse, both the mother-in-law and daughter-in-law were adamant that something had to be done in recompense. But as for what exactly needed to be done, they did not know.

Kali's grandmother once said, 'Devatha still resides in the hill in Karattur. It is enough if you make offerings of new clothes and pray to her. Gods cannot be angry with people for too long.' The astrologer also agreed with her.

Kali had scaled the hill several times as a young boy. He had wandered around there with other boys. But he knew nothing about the temple. He only knew that Karattaiyan and Maadhorubaagan took up either side of the hill. Every morning, before she had her food, his grandmother turned in the direction of the hill and prayed, 'Karattaiyan, Devatha.'

He went up the hill and spoke to the priest: 'We need to make offerings to Devatha.' The priest gave him an appraising look, and said, 'Who told you to?' Kali told him about his grandmother and the story she had narrated.

'Devatha is no one but Maadhorubaagan himself,' sermonized the priest. 'Only people who do not know that tell these stories. For hundreds of years, our family has been conducting rituals for the half-female god. Many saints have sung his praise, calling him "Mother God", "One Part

Woman", and so on. The male and female together make the world. To show that to us, the Lord stands here combined with the Goddess. In other temples, you would see separate shrines for Eeswaran and Ambal. But here they stand together as one. He has given her the left half of his body. It is only when we give half of ourselves—both body and mind—to the woman that we can be good husbands. Even though we are born male, we also have feminine qualities within us. Considering all this, elders have called him One Part Woman. There is no female without the male, and no male without the female. The world goes on only when they come together. Did you see the deity? The right side is Eeswaran; the left is Ambal. This is the only place where you get this vision. No matter how many names we address him by, they all refer to this Eeswaran. But the poor illiterate people call him Devatha. Some people even say this is Kannagi. What can one say about such ignorance? We just have to keep quiet, assured that everything is Eeswaran.'

At the end of the conversation, Kali gave the priest the fifty rupees he had asked for. Buying new clothes for the deity was a separate responsibility. Maadhorubaagan is male and female fused into one. What great pleasure it is to stay as one, body to body, forever! Only god gets to enjoy such great pleasure. Kali had to buy two kinds of clothes.

All his in-laws came for the ceremony. It was a great crowd. The expenses were huge too. When the preparations for the ritual were on, they walked around the temple. There was a small dip in the hill between the temple and the peak of the hill. This was a small forest with thorny bushes and trees that were perhaps several centuries old. The dense foliage reverberated with the furious chirping of a variety of birds. A long mountain rock formed a border around this little forest, lying like a giant serpent on guard. Kali was wonderstruck seeing such a forest at this altitude.

He and Muthu had played here as children. They would run up to the peak and touch the rock there. They'd leap around the slopes with the ease of wild goats and monkeys. But this forest had never before revealed itself as a separate entity to him. He had been one with it before. But as he grew older, he began seeing things as separate from himself. He now looked at the forest in great surprise.

Muthu must have felt the same way, for he said, 'We have roamed inside this. But I have never seen it this way.'

They looked around for a path to enter the forest. Birds and animals had forged a warren of paths through the forest. En route to the rock at the peak, a narrow path branched off and led into this jungle. Muthu and Kali entered it in great delight. A mongoose, alarmed by this sudden human presence, ran and hid under a bush. The path led directly to a tree. When they looked to the other side of the tree, they saw a huge reclining figure. Fear seized Kali and, holding Muthu's hand in a firm grip, he walked ahead.

It was an earthen goddess. Vermilion had been scattered all over her body, and her face was aglow with wrath. But there was a faint smile at the corners of her lips. He felt the smile revealed a defiance that said, 'What can you do to me?'

When he stood at her feet, she appeared to be lying there with the full confidence that the entire land was hers. Her arms and legs were as big as the trunks of trees. She had a round face, and her wide-open eyes met his in an unwavering stare. Even when Kali averted his gaze, he could still feel her eyes boring deep into him. Trying to shake off the fear the forest had induced in them, he said, 'What goddess is she?'

And they heard a voice: 'She is Devatha, our Mother, our goddess.'

For a moment, it felt as though the forest itself had spoken. But they turned to see that an elderly woman, carrying a pot, was walking down the narrow path towards the spot. She had two children with her. It was she who had answered Kali's question.

Around the earthen goddess were small rocks planted firmly in the ground and laid out in a circle. Beside these, in a concealed spot, were three pots and bags. Kali gathered that the elderly woman had come to make an offering of rice porridge to the goddess. The woman's ears were covered with jewellery.

'Our Devatha lies right here under the cool shade of the tree and with a stream nearby,' she said. 'But they try to keep her locked in the temple and pray. She roams freely around the forest. Can you confine her within walls? Our Mother lies right here, while they are just praying to plain rock.'

'Where are you from, ma?' asked Kali.

The children who had come with her started playing in the forest. They ran around, climbed the trees and jumped from them. Their laughter and chatter sounded like birdsong. The woman replied as she proceeded to get things ready for cooking the pongal: 'We are from the other bank, thambi. Ages ago, it was from here that we migrated. Even though we had to move away, seeking livelihood, our Mother refused to come. She told us very clearly that if we needed her we should come and see her here. So we come once a year like this, perform a ritual, offer pongal and eat. We have been told that our people used to live around this hill. When the forest was destroyed, they got scattered in different directions. Some people are able to visit during the chariot festival in the month of Aani. That's when they gather here. Otherwise, people like me only visit whenever we can. Now, some ten or fifteen of us have come. They have gone to the temple. But what do I have to see in the temple when my Mother lies here? So I came here to get this ready.'

It occurred to Kali that he too needed to pray and offer pongal to this goddess. This was Devatha, the goddess who had claimed a space for herself in this spot between the red rocks of the mountains. Reclining on the earth, she had even made a forest around herself. She was the goddess whose wrath had been invoked ages ago by the tribal girl's curse; she was still here, untouched by the ravages of time. He knelt at her feet. But then, shuddering at the thought that even a slight movement of her feet could hit him in the face, he backed off a little.

'Who conducts the prayers to this goddess?' he asked the old woman.

33

'How can we let anyone else carry out the prayers for our goddess? We do it by ourselves. Some of our people live in this town, too. One of them comes and conducts the prayers once a week. Wherever we are, we save five rupees a year and send it to him,' she said.

'I want to have a prayer conducted, mother,' he said.

'Do it with pleasure. Come one afternoon—any afternoon. The priest will be here. Ask him and do whatever you need to do. Remember, you should keep a trident and cut open a rooster and offer its blood. Those are the important things. If you wish, you can also join me today to partake in these offerings.'

Kali was no longer keen on the prayers the priest conducted in the temple on the hill. Nor did he care about the extra expenses. He was determined that it was Devatha to whom he wanted to make the offerings. Whatever he earned working hard in the fields got spent in such prayers and offerings. But it didn't matter. It was not as if he had children amongst whom to divide his earnings.

'All right, Amma. We will come in the afternoon,' he said and got ready to leave.

She said, 'By then the pongal will be ready. Do come and eat with us.'

When he nodded and left the place, he saw that the children were playing with a monkey on one of the trees. Usually he lamented the need to do whatever prayer whoever recommended, but the thought of doing one for Devatha truly filled his heart with peace.

six

The person who performed the prayers and rituals for Devatha worked in a warehouse loading and unloading sacks of produce. He did not give any elaborate list of things to be prepared for the ceremony. Nor did he take any money. In addition to the usual things needed for the offering, he asked Kali and Ponna to get red powder for about eight annas and to buy new cloth from the store in a small street at the foot of the hill. And also a rooster for sacrifice. Ponna and her sister made the pongal.

The priest decorated Devatha. She did not inspire fear in Kali like she had done the day before. Using a soft piece of cloth, the priest cleaned her gently. At that moment, the goddess could have been any woman from any of the local families lying on her back.

Kali and Muthu went to roam around the small forest. It was dense with neem and palai trees. There were also a few kondrai trees that had grown very tall and had their flowers hanging in bunches. The forest contained several paths, all as narrow as the lines on one's hands. You could reach the Devatha shrine from any direction.

'Machan,' said Kali, addressing Muthu fondly, 'please find a special spot in this forest too. It would be of use if we come again.'

Muthu laughed. 'Do you think no one would have done that already?' he said and pointed to what looked like a thick kasarali bush but had a clearing inside. They could see that men had been sitting there since a short while. There were some cards and a few empty bottles lying around.

'Man always needs such spaces, mapillai!' explained Muthu. 'He wanders around looking for them. Some succeed; others keep looking. Then there are those who are fearful of going there even if they do manage to find such a place.'

Kali moved away towards Devatha's shrine. What he found there was not an ordinary woman lying on the ground. He saw a woman dressed in red, and with red splattered all over her; he saw a woman blazing with wrath. By applying a little red to her eyes, the priest had made them glow with great ire. Kali and Muthu were speechless. The priest performed the ritual in silence. All they could hear was the sound of bells. When the offerings were made, Muthu brought out a small bottle of arrack. The priest had not mentioned it, but Muthu somehow knew. The priest slashed the rooster and let the blood flow at Devatha's feet.

Once the cooking was done, they all ate. The rooster had been cooked in a gravy. Kali's father-in-law did not come.

He never came to such events. So, it was only Kali, Ponna, his mother, mother-in-law, and his brother-in-law and his wife. But there was still a lot of food left over even after the priest had eaten. They had to finish all the food before they left. The priest went out of the forest and brought in a few beggars who lived in the rest houses there. They were happy to have their plates filled with food.

When they finally climbed down the hill, Ponna felt very satisfied.

Kali visited the shrine whenever he was on the hillside. For several months, no one changed the cloth they had offered Devatha. The priest had not taken even a penny from him. Kali felt that the curse of the tribal girl would have lifted by now.

Ponna, too, was full of hope after praying to Devatha. Her expectations were heightened in the months that followed. After every twenty days, she prayed, 'God, please fill my womb at least this month.' Even if there was a day's delay in her menstrual cycle, she was filled with excitement: 'This is it!' But if her cycle began the next day, the house looked as though someone had died in it. She didn't eat properly and just lay around. Kali had to go to his mother for food. Even after cutting open a rooster and satiating Devatha's thirst for revenge, nothing changed.

Whenever he went to the temple, he stood at Devatha's feet.

'Has your thirst been unquenched through the ages? It is not up to me to make you pull in your revenge-thirsty tongue. I am an ordinary man. For several births to come, I will do what I can. Please save me from being the talk of the town. I am unable to answer everyone's wretched questions. Ponna is wasting away. I am the one who is born in this useless lineage. Why are you avenging Ponna for that?' Saying this, he broke down in front of her.

But nothing quenched Devatha's anger.

seven

Sleep eluded Kali even after he had finished eating the snack. He lay on the cot in the cool shade of the portia tree, his eyes closed as he savoured the gentle breeze. He could hear the sounds of cooking from inside. After tossing and turning for a while, he sat up, and the cot creaked under him. The fast for the chariot festival and the snack that had followed—neither had given him any joy. Instead, his mind was flooded with all sorts of thoughts that confused him.

Kali thought he might feel better if he went out for a stroll into the forest with Muthu. Where was Muthu? Was it a workday in the fields? Muthu was good at finding or creating new secret spots—havens that were unknown to anyone else.

Kali remembered that the last time he visited, Muthu took him to the well. There was very little water in it.

'How can we swim in this, machan?' Kali asked.

'You have known me for all these years, and yet how little you know me! Would I take you for a swim in this? Come,

come and see. You will be amazed,' said Muthu, climbing down the stairs into the well.

It was a deep well. All rock. Kali wondered at the difficulty people must have faced in bursting so much rock and digging so deep. The steps went straight down, flattened out at a point into a landing, and then continued further down. Standing on that landing, Muthu looked up. In the light that streamed in, he could neither see anyone's head nor its shadow. 'Mapillai, be careful!' he shouted. Then, reaching out and gripping a rock on the other side of the downward staircase, he suddenly vanished into a gap in the wall. Although Kali was very used to roughing it out, he hesitated to follow Muthu into the dark hole.

Muthu peeped out from the hole and said, 'Hold on to that rock that is sticking out. Do you see that little groove wide enough just to place your foot there? Don't be scared. Even if you fall, it will only be into the well. And there is water enough to not get hurt.'

Moving like an iguana that clutches tight even the smallest of surfaces, Kali entered the opening in the rock. Only then did he realize that it was not just a hole but a big cave with a rocky floor and a sand-plastered roof. Kovai creepers fell like a curtain, covering the entrance to the cave. Kali was amazed. Muthu had enough things stocked up there to throw a feast. Muthu started skinning the two white rats he had caught that day and brought hanging from a string on his waist. One was a male with swollen balls and the other was a female. Together, they'd make a decent amount of meat.

The cave had everything—a penknife, a stove made with small stones, an earthen pot, wood. There was even a little money stowed away. Muthu pounded some chillies and roasted the meat. How did he manage to get wood that burnt without smoke? Even if someone were drawing water from the well, they wouldn't know anyone was down here in the cave. Kali stretched his legs and lay down. The tasty meat went well with the arrack. The little bit of gravy at the bottom was incredibly delicious. Kali poured it into the curve of his palm and slurped it down. They both drank, ate and slept there undisturbed for several hours and emerged only in the evening.

'Only snakes use the holes in wells, don't they?' asked Kali.

'I have calamus to ward off real snakes,' replied Muthu. 'Its fragrance repels them. And if we smoke samburani as soon as we finish eating, the smell of the meat won't linger.'

Kali said, 'No man can discover such a place. You are the snake!'

That place must still be a secret. If anyone found out, Muthu would immediately change his hideout. But who was going to climb down that well? Even if someone did, they would need extraordinary eyes to see past the screen of kovai creepers. How many hours would he have worked inside? Muthu's work was better than even those of professional roof-layers. He had done such a perfect job.

It would be nice if he were here now.

Kali sat up. Seeing this, Ponna came running. 'Maama, do you want water?' He nodded. She ran in. Whenever they were here, Ponna was more sensitive to each and every move of his and paid close attention to his every little need. Sometimes it looked like she was lost in some other work, but her mind was fully occupied with him.

Her mother once remarked, 'As if you have some wonder of a husband that no one else has! Even if he moves his finger a little bit, you run and stand in front of him.'

'That's right. My husband is a wonder for me,' she replied.

'Let's see if you still run around taking care of your husband after a child is born,' said her mother.

'Even if I give birth to ten children, he will always be my first child,' she responded, brimming with pride.

'It is all right to desire. But you are greedy. Maybe that's what has put off even the gods,' her mother said with a sigh.

The conversation ended there, and silence fell.

Now, when Ponna brought Kali an aluminium pitcher full of water, he drained it in a single gulp.

She laughed, 'Were you this thirsty?'

He was about to say, 'Yes, but it is definitely less than Devatha's thirst,' but he stopped himself. Perhaps because that was the day the deity went back to the hill, all his thoughts revolved around that one event.

'When is your brother coming?' he said to her.

Ponna said, 'He went somewhere in the morning and has not returned yet. But he'll be here in time to eat. Today it's your favourite: drumstick.'

Kali's lips widened into a smile, but his heart was not in it; his mind was elsewhere. He felt that if he made Ponna lie next to him, embraced her tightly and cushioned his head on her breasts, all his broodings would vanish. In the middle of the day, in the shadow of the tree . . . Why was his mind stuck on impossible things? He held her hand and gently rubbed it against his cheek. But then her mother called from inside. Had her sister-in-law been at home, there wouldn't have been so much work for Ponna. But she, along with her child, had gone to her mother's house. They had been invited to keep the fast there.

Kali kept looking at Ponna as she crossed the threshold and entered the house. The things she had done in the hope of getting a child! She would do whatever was asked of her. Everyone had been patient for six months after the wedding. But there had been innuendoes even before that. Then they started asking direct questions. The only way to save oneself was to conceive in the first month of marriage. Otherwise, the interrogation would begin in some form or another. His mother, who was patient for six months, started her treatments soon after that.

She kept a watch on Ponna's menstrual cycle that month. As soon as it came to pass, she told Ponna to drink the juice of some shoots on the morning of the third day. She said forcefully, 'Don't eat anything else even by mistake. The juice will be bitter. You will have to close your eyes and swallow it.' After that, Ponna got used to eating different shoots and drinking different potions. Her tongue became numb to all the bitterness. The goal was to beget a child, and she was ready to do anything to attain that goal. The bitterness of the medication paled in comparison. But her mother-in-law's medication didn't go down all that easily.

Before Ponna woke up and stepped out, her mother-in-law was busy crushing a big bunch of tender neem leaves. It made Ponna retch. At her own parents' home, she would throw a fit even when her mother made her take regular medicine. Her mother would yell, 'Am I asking you to eat neem shoots?' But now she was having to eat neem shoots for real. It made her very angry at her mother-in-law.

'Should I put a child on her lap the month after the wedding? I can only drop a grinding stone into her lap. Can't she be patient for a year or two? We are young. She is unable to see us enjoy a few good years without hassles like children. She can't bear to see me happy.'

Kali smiled and said, 'It is only neem juice, right? All the worms in your stomach will die.'

'You mother wants a worm to crawl in my womb. And you are saying it will die. Are you two playing with me?' And she punched him in his chest.

'Ah, it feels like you are throwing flowers at me. Please punch me more, darling,' he pleaded. But he didn't say that she needn't drink the bitter extract.

His mother extracted the juice out of the crushed neem shoots by filtering them through a pure white cloth. It gave very little juice. After repeating the process some three or four times, she got a quarter cup of the extract. She had somehow procured a measuring cup that was normally used in wedding rituals; she cleaned it and got it ready overnight.

She poured the neem extract into that vessel and closed the lid. She then asked Ponna to come after pouring water over herself fully clad in a sari. After that, Ponna had to stand, dripping wet, facing east in front of the house. Dawn was appearing, waving its raised hand to everyone. 'Pray,' she said to Ponna. She too prayed.

'O you who are travelling west,' she said, addressing the sun as she prayed out loud. 'She is drinking this so that my lineage will endure. Please let it grow,' said her mother-in-law. Ponna murmured something to herself.

Kali's mother had invited a white-sari-clad distant relative, a grandmother. She must have been a hundred years old, but other than her cataract-covered eyes, she looked fine. She had seven or eight children and a drove of grandchildren. Ponna's mother-in-law too was a widow. But, for some reason, she was not supposed to hand over the earthen bowl of medicine to Ponna. To receive something from a woman in white is like receiving something from the goddess herself. The old woman lifted the bowl above her head, prayed to the dawn and gave it to Ponna.

'Don't think about anything, dear one. Close your eyes and just gulp it down. The gods will open their eyes,' she said. Ponna did as told.

Even though she drank it up very fast, it was bitter beyond belief. The vessel was heavy too. She retched and gagged, but didn't stop drinking. When she was done, her mother-in-law put a handful of jaggery into her mouth. But the bitterness did not leave her palate for a week. No worm crawled in her belly either. She was taken here and there, and was told that she was being given medicines to conceive. But nothing worked.

She had laughed once, whispering into Kali's double-curve-studded ears, 'If you had married a goat instead of me, it would have given birth to a litter by now for all the shoots she must have eaten.'

Stony-faced, he had replied, 'I should have been born a male goat for that.' Even now, thinking of that made her smile till her eyes welled up with tears.

eight

In the matter of offering prayers, Kali and Ponna left no stone unturned. They did not discriminate between small and big temples. They promised an offering to every god they encountered. For the forest gods, it was a goat sacrifice. For the temple gods, it was pongal. For some gods, the promises even doubled. If a child were indeed born, the rest of their lives would be spent in fulfilling these promises. Kali, in fact, was ready to forgo his cattle and all that he had saved with his incredible frugality, if only their prayers would bear fruit. But no god seemed to pay heed.

How many prayers and promises they must have made in Karattur alone! If you went past the forest where the Devatha shrine is, and climbed further up, you would arrive at the Dandeeswarar temple on top. They called this deity the Pillayar on the hilltop. He was guarding the maladikkal, the barren rock that was nearby. An ordinary soul could not reach there; one needed both mental and physical strength.

When they were younger, Kali and Muthu went there with a large crowd of young men on every new-moon day without fail. People would arrive there in bullock carts. Elderly folk and ailing people would touch the first step and pray and lie down in their carts.

Muthu and Kali's crowd of young men positioned themselves in the mandapams, the rest houses that marked every significant climb, and laughed at those who needed to rest before proceeding further. They would make a competition of running up the steps. It was pretty much like running on flat ground. It was only after the dip at Pambar Pallam that it got steep. One had to be patient, particularly while climbing down. If not, then one ran the risk of tumbling down the hill, without any control, all the way till the hollow landing. The young crowd usually left their homes before the crack of dawn, walking and running to reach the hill six or seven miles away. To cross distances was a sport. Nothing gave them as much joy as this.

People sold millet rice in the mandapams on the hill. The rice was mixed with thick yogurt and was full of the fragrance of millets. Two full pitchers were enough to keep hunger at bay. Besides, they were of an age when they didn't worry about hunger. In fact, going to the temple was only a feeble excuse to undertake this journey. It was over as soon as they stood in the inner sanctum, touched the camphor flame, prayed and smeared the holy ash on their foreheads.

No one went into the forest where the Devatha shrine was. A fear of that place had been instilled in everyone. On days when there were bigger crowds, they even appointed someone to make sure no one strayed into the forest. Walking past it, they came to a rocky patch where small trees grew out of the crevices between the rocks. They were so narrow, no one could walk through them. So instead they jumped from rock to rock. The ruckus they made leaping about like this scattered even the monkeys away.

Then a flat surface. If you walked over it, keeping to the left side, you would come to a gigantic rock that stood like a sickle. Its tip looked like it was ready to pierce the sky. They would place their feet on small fissures and climb to the top of even this rock. There was a cave under this rock. It was cold inside. They'd lie down there. If no one was talking, they could fall asleep. If they leaned out from the entrance to the cave, they could see the town below. They could even see the other temple located at the base of the hill and the thatched roofs of the stationary chariots. The houses of the priests who worked in the temple, and other houses, were all arranged along four or five streets. The temple tank appeared large and spread out. The two temple tanks would look like beggars' bowls that held sand. Running right across from the temple at the base of the hill was the devadasis' lane. Anyone was allowed into that lane.

In front of the cave was a vast shaded space. They would talk non-stop. Now when he tried to remember what they talked about, Kali could not recollect a thing. Perhaps such incessant chatter was the prerogative of youth alone. Once he grew up, the brain might have decided that it was all meaningless and erased all memory of that prattle. But it could do nothing to the feelings of happiness that came with it. They were spread out like a vast, open space.

When the sun went down a bit, they'd move from that spot and go towards the next peak. How many peaks there were in those hills! They had to climb down from the rock that was right in front of the cave. In the gap that looked like a crocodile's gaping jaws, there was a stream. On rainy days, they could jump, dunk their heads in and bathe in it. For the elderly folk who managed to limp, wobble and drag themselves to that spot, it was sacred water. 'Don't go into the water!' they'd shout. Above that, they had to climb on to a barren rock surface that was totally bereft of any vegetation. No tree, shrub or creeper could grow on that bald rock. That was where they could feel the force of the wind. Wind is more powerful than anything else. If it sets its mind to it, it can destroy anything in an instant. They could climb only after humbly requesting the wind to give them way. They had to place their feet carefully, their grip tenacious and strong like an iguana's, and focus on climbing one step at a time. In certain spots, the only way to move was to crawl over the rock like a creeper. And there was nothing the buoyancy of youth was not equal to.

From that spot, the Dandeeswarar temple seemed like a small lookout on top of the hill. Right next to it was a stone that was as tall as a human being. That was the maladikkal, the barren rock. On the other side of the rock, it looked like someone had carved a semicircle out of the hillside. The challenge was to come round that semicircular path.

Even if you leaned over a little, you would start shivering in fear; your soles would sweat and you'd fall and vanish down the steep hillside. It was sport for them to perform feats on that spot. Several people had died trying to walk around the maladikkal, in the hope of fulfilling some wish or having their prayers answered. Due to this mounting death toll, a British man had built a wall that barricaded the stone. But could anyone change a belief that had survived through the ages?

In fact, the wall made it all the more convenient. One could hold the edge of the wall and move quickly to the other side. Then, relying on the coarse surface of the rock, one could cross the semicircle and get to the other side of the rock. After that, you could hold on to its edge and proceed further. If you were used to it, you could go around it in the blink of an eye. Kali and Muthu had done this many times.

But men don't benefit from this prayer. Only women do.

That is what Ponna was told by a short old woman who had come one day to weed their field of groundnuts. According to her, any woman would be blessed with a child if she walked around the barren rock. She added that that was how she too had conceived. Ponna listened intently to all this before leaving for the temple with all that she needed to make a pongal offering. She did not listen to anything Kali said. She did not want to tell anyone where they were going. They might discourage them from going. Everyone would have an opinion. While beginning to walk around the barren rock, even if someone warned 'Careful! Careful!' it could be distracting. Also, if Ponna felt scared on seeing the spot, she might return without walking around the rock. In that case, if someone came along, it might give them something humiliating to talk about. 'She said she would walk around the stone, but she took one look at it and came back without doing it,' they'd snicker for ages. People constantly needed something to gossip about.

They went on a day when it was not crowded on the hill. Ponna had never been to the top where the maladikkal was. She had noticed it when people had pointed to the Dandeeswarar temple and the stone that looked like a raised finger and told her that was it. She was used to roaming in the fields. The only hurdle to negotiating a bald rock that had no steps was her sari. But since no one seemed to be around, she lifted her sari up to her knees, tucked it in, and climbed with ease. When they reached the cave, Kali pointed out the barren rock to her. It looked to her as though someone had stood a gigantic, flat rock upright and placed a small knot of hair on top of it. Kali tightly embraced Ponna, who sat and leisurely gazed at the stone. He pulled the sari away from her breasts and buried his head between them like a goat kid. He held her passionately, nuzzling her, when she lowered her face to his head knot and said, 'Maama, are you scared I might fall while walking round the stone? Is that why you are giving it to me now like this was the last time?'

Kali let go of his embrace in shock. Tear trails ran all over her face. The altitude of the hills, the shade of the trees and the flat ground there had kindled his lust. Her sari, which had now gone up to her knees, and the cloth covering her breasts, which had come undone in the wind, all added to his longing. The sacred thread caressing her neck and the taali glittered invitingly. He was never satisfied making love in the confines of a walled space. He preferred open spaces. He had to see the sky. It was even better if a bird took a peep on its way somewhere. He would take her to their barnyard just for this.

The two-acre farm had a fence but no roof. As soon as he set the cot down in the middle, he was in the mood. She would have some complaint or another: 'The goat is watching; now it is the cow.' She quite liked it, but would still make mild protests because she did not want him to think of her as a shameless woman.

He would say, 'Don't we see when the cows and goats do it? Now let them watch us.'

'You have no decency at all, maama!' she would reply.

Whenever he managed to find good arrack, he took her to the farm without fail. She did not like toddy. She complained that the sour burp stank for days. All she needed was half a glass of arrack that had a sharp sting on her tongue.

Now, the hillside had awoken the same desires in Kali. But she put out his fire with just that one remark.

She immediately tried to console him. 'We are here to pray, maama. That's why it came out like that.'

'Whatever it is, don't say such crazy things,' he said.

They made peace and climbed to the spot where the barren rock was. One look at the foot-wide space around it and she was scared.

'We don't have to do it if you are scared,' he said.

The old woman had said, 'Don't look outside. As long as you keep looking at the stone as you walk around it, you will have no trouble. It is just like walking on a ridge in the fields. The difference is that there you would fall into the mud if you skidded, and here, it is rock—if your head hits it, it will shatter into smithereens like a coconut. But it is nothing for those who are used to walking around in the fields and forests, Ponna.'

All the stuff she had brought to make pongal with lay in front of Dandeeswarar. Only those who planned to walk around the stone made the pongal offering. Others just lit camphor and prayed. They had bought all the stuff with the intention of making the pongal once Ponna finished the walk. But now Kali was worried, wondering if she'd be able to do it. Even if she tripped a little, that was the end of it all. What if something like that happened? They would definitely accuse him of doing away with her by pushing her off the edge. This place was infamous for murders and suicides. But it did not appear that anyone who went to walk praying for fertility ever fell down. But what if it happened to Ponna? His heart suddenly weighed like a rock. If she fell, he would fall down with her too. It might even be possible to live without her. But he couldn't live with the allegations.

'Maama, I will walk around now. If something happens to me, don't let it affect you for long. Marry another woman. At least let her be blessed with a child,' Ponna said with teary eyes.

'Chee!' he exclaimed, dismissing her gloomy words. Wiping the tears from her eyes, he consoled her, 'We lack in nothing. We can be happy. It doesn't matter if we don't have a child. How long will these morons in the village keep harassing us? Maybe for another ten or twelve years. By then we would have grown old. So what if we don't have children? We can still triumph. We can write off the little land we have to some temple. Or else, we can leave it to someone who has nothing. Let him make a living out of it.'

He embraced her. He felt his mind had acquired some clarity. But she was confident about completing her walk around the stone. She took this as a challenge above all the other prayers she had endured until then. Her logic was that the gods might find some compassion for her if she put herself through this most difficult of tests. Once she made up her mind to go ahead with it, Kali told her how to. He felt she might fly into a wild panic if he offered to show her how to negotiate the precipice. So he simply showed her. He went to the edge of the wall and said to her, 'Look,' and in just two swift moves went around the stone, and climbed over the other wall. When she screamed, 'Maama!' he was already in front of her, laughing.

Everything felt like an illusion. She wondered why such a simple thing scared her so much. Kali was clearly used to walking around the stone. Her brother, Muthu, too had done this enough number of times. But no one at home knew this. Young men are great at keeping secrets. The second time, he asked her to watch closely, and demonstrated it again with her permission. She observed how to hold on to the railing and also made a note of how much space there was to place her feet. It reminded her of a rock lizard. The way his body clung to the rock while his arms and legs were spread out embracing it looked just like what a rock lizard would do.

He told her she could either walk around once or do it three times, and went ahead and did three rounds himself. Watching him, Ponna lost all her fears. Like the old woman had said, this was nothing for someone who had roamed around forests. He helped her hoist up her sari and fasten it securely.

Two vultures circled around in the endless expanse of the sky. They seemed motionless, their wings stretched wide without a discernible flutter. They blessed her. She held her palms together over her head and prayed, 'God, my father, please make sure I do not gain the reputation for being barren.' And just like he had done, she crossed the wall and navigated the precipice with the tenacity of a rock lizard. When she reached the end of her ordeal, he gave her a hand and helped her cross over the wall to his side. He held her close to his heart and exultantly kissed her on the cheek, lips and head. When they sat in front of Dandeeswarar, she burst into sobs.

'Seeking a life, we have pawned our lives. Don't cheat us, god,' she cried out loud. With her head on his chest, she felt dizzy. She lay there with her eyes closed. He laid her on the ground and splashed some water on her face. She regained consciousness. 'Maama, shall I do two more rounds?' she said.

He was firm in his refusal. The effect was the same whether you did it once or a thousand times.

She started making pongal in front of the Dandeeswarar temple. This temple had different priests. They came only when there were crowds, like on new-moon days. On other days, they came only if someone went and fetched them. Kali climbed down fast and was back by the time she had finished making the pongal. She was amazed at his speed. When the mind is excited, the body begins to take flight. By the time the priest came and finished the prayers and they climbed back down, darkness had begun to wrap itself around everything.

They could never forget the night that followed. That was the night everything came together blissfully. That was the night they slept well, confident that the seed they'd planted would definitely grow. She also thought of it as her penance for wounding his heart with her words earlier that day. His body and mind expressed his conviction that nothing could sufficiently express his gratitude for this woman who had risked her life doing something all women feared to do. The night was filled to the brim with giving and receiving. In the middle of the farm, on the coir-rope cot, she lay like a garland on his chest. They both felt they needed nothing; nothing could make him happier than to die at such a moment.

She was confident that she wouldn't bleed that month, that there would finally be an end to all the talk.

nine

A nd the kind of talk they had endured! Many people had concluded that Ponna and Kali would not be able to have children at all. It was, in fact, their desire that it should not happen. Even her sister-in-law said so once.

'What are you going to do by saving money? Eat well, wear good clothes and be happy.'

'Why? Are we starving now? Are we standing naked in front of your house?' Ponna retorted.

Her sister-in-law's face shrank. 'I didn't mean it that way.'

'What kind of talk is this? Shit-eater talk.' Ponna could not keep it from tumbling out.

And her sister-in-law held on to that last comment. She went around telling everyone, 'She called me a shit-eater.' No one bothered to ask what had provoked such an abuse. 'Ponna talks too much,' they said. But Muthu would never say anything like that. He loved his brother-in-law more than his sister. He scolded his wife. And all of this effectively ruined the relationship between the sisters-in-law. They never again spoke to each other properly. Whenever she knew

Ponna was coming, her sister-in-law left for her mother's house with her child.

Kali had two uncles. They lived quite well in Thalaiyur with a field and a house. But they had an eye on his property. Whenever his uncles' wives met him at any function, they fawned over him like they were ready to hand over their lives to him on a platter. The uncles visited them at least once a month. They brought fruits and vegetables or something else for their sister, Kali's mother. They gave some of it to her and the rest to Ponna. Ponna always made fun of this practice: 'Even when she is fit to be a grandmother, she gets her due from her mother's house.'

Kali would smile but not say anything.

One of the uncles had three daughters and a son. The other one had two sons. Once in a while, they would send their children over and it was not easy to attend to them. But all of this was not out of love for Kali and Ponna. Rather, this idea of bonding regularly was a strategic move on the part of the uncles. After all, if it ever came to a property dispute later, the closer ones might get more, right?

The second uncle's last son was Kadhirvel. In his village, everyone called him 'Water Gourd'. He looked like a water gourd on which someone had hung a shirt. It was easier to assemble a herd of goats than to keep an eye on him. One moment he'd be playing right in front of the house and the next second he couldn't be seen. How long could one keep an eye on him like a snake upon its prey? Looking for him, Ponna would have to walk up and down between the house and the farm at least four times a day. But if there was work in the field, Kali expected her to be there. Water Gourd was good at wandering alone, and she let him do as he wished. It was all right as long as he did not create trouble.

The children did bizarre things when they jumped and played in the well. When one of the boys wanted to leave early and started climbing up the well, they would throw mud on him. He would have to jump back into the water to wash away all that mud. It was very difficult to escape the mud-pelting. During one such game, our Water Gourd fellow threw a stone at the boy who pelted him with mud. It hit him sharply on his feet and he writhed in pain. But he retaliated by aiming one back at Water Gourd. It was sharp as a sickle and it hit our boy on the back of his head, even making a dent in it. Despite his dense hair, blood flowed down his nape. It stopped only after a herb extract was applied on it for a week.

As soon as she heard the news, his mother came rushing like a she-devil. God knows who managed to convey the news to her three villages away and into a forest beyond that. There are folks who go out of their way, first thing in the morning, to make sure they have a nice fight to watch. Shouldn't the woman have first inquired about what had happened? She might have a great deal of love for her child, but how was any of this Ponna's fault? She was screaming even as she came down the street. When she reached the gate, her words were as hot as the sun: 'She would know only if she had a child of her own! She has taken such good care that my boy's head is broken. Would any mother allow that to happen?'

When the boy had come home injured, Ponna had run here and there to find a medicine to apply on his wound. All that seemed to mean nothing to his mother. All that Water Gourd had done when he was bleeding profusely was to whimper in pain. But now, looking at his mother, he wailed. His mother spoke as if it was Ponna who had deliberately thrown a stone at him. Disgusted with the behaviour of the mother and son, Ponna retorted, 'Well, if you know the blessing of having a child, why don't you keep him to yourself? Why send him here?'

That was it! A thousand words came pouring forth then.

'Do you think we are the kind of people who wash their asses in any river?' raged the boy's mother. 'I sent him because he wanted to go to his aunt's place. Look at her, advising me like she has raised some seven or eight children.'

Ponna did not say anything. With the entire village watching, Ponna's mother-in-law rushed to her sister-in-law and said in a pleading voice, 'Please leave him here. I will take care of him.' But the woman didn't listen. She took her son away.

Long after she was gone, her words seemed to echo in Ponna's ears. Kali did not say anything. Ponna cried, 'Even if we don't have children and decide to give away our money, we should give nothing to these people.' He just smiled. Since then, neither of the uncles sent their children there.

This asset of theirs, the land, seemed to irk everyone. Does anyone know who ploughed this land a hundred years ago? Can anyone say whose land it would be a hundred years from now? If man had the prospect of living any longer than he already did, he would want to keep everything for himself. When we finally leave, life strips us even of the little piece of cloth we are wearing. And all this talk! Even those who look like they could die any day now talk non-stop about money and inheritance.

One Tuesday, Ponna went to the fair with Pottupaatti. The woman had got her name from the large pottu, larger than her forehead, that was tattooed on her. Ponna needed company to walk the five or six miles and though Pottupaatti was terribly slow, Ponna asked her to join her.

Covering her head with a basket, Ponna tackled the sun as she walked. Their onward journey was smooth. She bought enough stuff to last a week. She even got titbits like pears and puffed rice with peanuts. Her basket was full. The old woman had no money on her. Feeling bad for her, Ponna bought her some puffed rice with peanuts for one anna and dropped it in her basket. On the way back, the woman remarked casually, 'You have bought so little. Do you have a child crying at home? Your husband and you are protecting an inheritance that god knows which wretched dogs will claim later. Why don't you eat what you like? Whom are you being so miserly for? A woman without her husband and an inheritance without an heir are the same, they say.'

Ponna was enraged. She had taken pity on the old woman, but now she started shooting her mouth off.

'You and your husband had no control and you were

producing babies even when you were forty-five. You divided your land among them. Do any of your sons work the land now? Didn't it go as bad as not having heirs? You don't even have anyone to give you some money to go to the fair. You don't have money even to buy yourself some puffed rice. What have you accomplished by bearing children?'

Ponna made sure the woman heard each word clearly and stomped off. The woman could not say anything. She was perhaps scared that if she said anything more Ponna might knock her down. But she spoke to others once she reached the village. 'Do you know what happened when I went to the fair with that witch?' she began and told the entire village her tale of woe. In her version, the old woman had caringly suggested that Ponna should buy some snacks for her husband. To which, apparently, Ponna had replied, 'It is because of your careless spending that you lost all your land. Both your property and mine are properties with no heir.' All of it came to Ponna's ears. Neither Pottupaatti nor her daughter-in-law spoke to Ponna after that. Ponna thought it best not to say anything more.

It seemed that people who had children could do anything they wanted—that only *they* had such rights. But Ponna was aware of her sharp tongue and what it could unleash at any moment. Fearing the consequences of such an outburst, she tried to be very careful in public spaces. But, somehow or the other, a quarrel would ensue. Even her neighbour Sarasa had a silly expectation that Ponna should bequeath things to her children. After all, Ponna herself had none.

Sarasa's children happily helped themselves to kuzhambu, rasam and anything from Ponna's house. Sometimes, she even made them eat there. If not for the chatter of those children, she would only have to listen to her own echo bouncing off the walls. So, she was very loving towards them. The older girl played snakes and ladders and hopscotch with Ponna. Then they'd both comb their hair and decorate it with flowers. The girl didn't even mind running small errands for Ponna.

It so happened that Sarasa's brother-in-law was getting married. The girl was from Kallur, which was just two villages away. Sarasa had insisted that Ponna come ahead of time. But since it involved getting a bunch of other women ready, Ponna got delayed. How could Ponna go all that distance alone? Some ten or fifteen of them went together. In front of everybody, Sarasa made a derisive remark. Perhaps it was her way of showing how close she was to Ponna.

'Despite my telling you to come early, you are arriving only now. Did you get delayed in getting your daughters ready?'

She was showing off that she had children while Ponna didn't. Her mocking tone stung her. One or two of the women laughed at Sarasa's remark and looked at Ponna.

'As if those with children are always doing such a great job!' Ponna exploded. Unable to stop herself, she went on, 'This one runs around with a soiled ass after shitting, the other one runs about wiping its mouth after eating. I comb this one's hair every day. It is not enough to give birth to children—you should also know how to take care of them!'

65

Silence prevailed for a while in the entire wedding pandal. The women who had laughed at Sarasa's remark were not laughing now. Ponna did not feel like staying there any longer. She turned around at the entrance and started walking back. To make sure she didn't give anyone a chance to come after her, she walked really fast and crossed that village. She later heard that Sarasa had sat and cried about it. She might have done it to clear her name.

After this episode, Ponna did not attend any functions. Whether weddings or funerals, either Kali or his mother had to go. If any of them put pressure on Ponna, she would respond in their own style: 'I have no children. What function is going to happen in my house tomorrow? Whom am I going to invite with betel leaf and nut? Are things so bad that when I die no one would come to carry me? Will they let me just lie here and rot? I don't want to go anywhere. And no one needs to come here either. It is enough if they leave me alone.'

Sarasa pulled a long face for a while. She even kept her children from going to Ponna's. And she also took better care of them—she washed their feet, fed them well and combed their hair properly. Ponna smiled inside watching all this. But it lasted just a week. Then everything went back to where it was. The older girl started coming running to Ponna with a comb in her hand. Sarasa too squeezed in a word or two here and there. But Ponna was sure that Sarasa's dream of getting a share of their property for her children must have vanished.

Ponna had believed that the barren rock would put an end to all the cruel talk. But all that effort of climbing up the hill and putting her life at risk came to naught. No change occurred in her body. Everything went on just as it had. She didn't know what more could be done.

ten

An ant in his armpit woke Kali up from his slumber. The skin swelled up a little when he rubbed it involuntarily. He sat up. Sounds of cooking were coming from inside the house. Muthu hadn't returned yet. Kali felt like going for a short walk. Other than the house and the portia tree, there was mainly sun-scorched dry land all around. It had been twenty days since the month of Aani had begun, but the sky hadn't yet opened its eyes to shed tears of rain. The farmers were waiting for the rain so they could begin the first round of ploughing. But while the heat kept rising, not a single smudge of grey could be spotted in the sky. It sowed within them the fear that the rains might fail this year.

There was no problem of fodder for the cattle. One granary of pulses and another of corn were still intact. Water scarcity might hit them, but whatever water was left in the well could be used sparingly—none for the coconut trees, only for the cattle. After all, it would have to rain at least by Aipasi or Karthigai. The god in Thattangadu had apparently prophesied this: 'There will be less rain this year for sure!' Kali thought he should plan accordingly.

He looked up. The sun was overhead. It must be around noon. He wondered if his mother would have given water to the cows. He had put the husk in the shed. The cows only needed to be brought and tethered. His mother would do the work for one or two days, but he was contented only when he did it all himself. He wondered why he could not trust anyone. Ponna always scolded him, 'I too am a farmer's daughter. Don't you think I can handle them for a day? What is it that you do to them that I don't?' At night, even a little movement from them would wake him up. It had been several years since he had slept peacefully. Even when the body is ready for deep rest, the mind keeps irking it just like the ant from this tree. How can one sleep like that?

The barnyard occupied his mind wherever he was. It was only there that he felt safe. It was enough just to be there and talk to the cattle. When he was alone in the fields, someone would come at night to keep him company. Whenever Uncle Nallayyan came, Kali was delighted. He was a distant relative of Kali's and must have been over fifty. And he always spoke with great excitement.

Uncle Nallayyan never married. It was all because of what had happened in his youth. He did not get along with his father. They stayed in the same house, but they tried not to see each other. He found his father's voice as bitter as neem fruit. The moment he heard it, he would run far away. When asked what exactly the problem was, he smiled as he explained,

'When I was a child, he took me on his shoulders to see the temple chariot. Everything would have been fine had he come straight back home after seeing the chariot. Instead, he went to the devadasis' street, carrying me along. He sat me down on the porch and went inside one of the houses. I waited for a while, but it seemed like the man was not going to be out soon. So I walked back home on my own. I must have been five or six years old. Did I keep quiet about this at home? No. I told my mother that it happened like this, like that, and so on. Even my mother did not mind the fact that the little child had walked all that distance alone. She took umbrage only to the fact that he went to a devadasi. He came long after I had returned and said, "The boy got lost in the crowds. There is nowhere I haven't looked for him. That is all our bad luck." My mother rushed towards him with a broomstick and hit him on the head. She screamed, "You want a devadasi? If you come into the house again, I will chew off your neck." It appears that my mother never allowed him near her after that. That made him angry at me. Whenever he saw me, he would grimace like he'd just drunk some castor oil. As for me, I could never forget how he sat me down at the entrance to the devadasi's house and vanished inside. So, we don't get along.'

When Nallayyan was fifteen or sixteen years old, the father and son got into a massive fight. Standing in the field, his father threw a ball of sand at him, and in response he threw the spade at his father. It cut into his father's calf and the old man collapsed, screaming, 'Aiyo!' Scared that he would be caught, Uncle Nallayyan ran to the house and took money from his mother's purse, which she kept hidden inside a pot. He then ran away from the village and did not come back for six months. When they finally got over their anger at his stealing the money, they looked for him here and there, but they could not find him.

Six months later, early one morning, when his mother stepped outside the house, she saw her son sleeping there. She made a huge scene. He could not answer any questions about where he went and what he did. He had grown dark and gaunt. But within a week he improved a little in his mother's care.

'I cannot believe I named this wretched dog the "good" one,' his father murmured, brooding over what 'nalla' in 'Nallayyan' meant. 'I should hit my own head with a slipper. A dog that steals from his own home can even drop a rock on your head while you sleep,' he fumed.

Uncle said to his mother, 'Is your husband suggesting that I go steal from other people's homes?'

When others asked his father about the son, he would say, 'That barbarian was not born to me. Who knows for which bastard she dropped her clothes to beget this one?' But he made sure he didn't say any of this within his wife's hearing. He could never forgive his son for earning him the reputation that he sat his own child outside a devadasi's house and went in.

After that, it became a routine for Uncle Nallayyan to run away every two months or so. The moment anyone said anything even remotely hurtful, he ran away. No one knew where he went and what he did. 'Where will that wretched dog go? He must be outside some restaurant, feeding on leftovers,' his father would say. Once Uncle gained the reputation for being unstable, no one was willing to offer their daughter in marriage to him. Even after all his younger brothers were married, they could not find a girl for him. 'I don't want to earn the sin of wrecking a girl's life,' said his father and abandoned the search for a bride for his son. But his mother never stopped ranting.

Uncle himself did not care for marriage. When he shaved off his beard and moustache, his mother sang a dirge and made such a scene as though someone had died:

Your first shave,
your becoming a bridegroom,
I thought these eyes would see and tear up.
This is no first shave,
and you are no bridegroom,
you roamed aimlessly
and have tired, dark eyes.
What do I do? What do I do?

But Uncle was not the kind to be moved by such dirges. He hugged his mother, wiped away her tears and said, 'What did you accomplish by getting married? You spread your pallu for a worthless husband, gave birth to so many children, and you are suffering till today. Drop the matter. I don't need to go through the same hell.'

Kali, lying on the cot in his farm and listening to these old stories, said, 'Where all did you go, Uncle? Look at me. I am reluctant even to leave this spot and go to the fair once a week. I feel it is good to be contented with this barnyard and the field. Where did you go for three or six months at a stretch?

'Kalippa,' Uncle replied, 'the world is endless. It stretches on and on. On my way, if I got lost and wandered a bit, it would appear that I was returning to where I started from. In those moments, I hated our village. When the money in hand was all spent and I had nowhere else to go, I would come back home very reluctantly.'

He was the not the kind to open up and give words to his feelings. But the barnyard made even Uncle Nallayyan say, 'Kalippa, when I lie here in your farm, it feels as comforting as lying in my mother's womb.' That was exactly the way Kali felt about his barnyard.

He always slept in the farm. Even in summer, he laid his cot out in the open. During the monsoons and in winter, the cot would lie inside the shed. His was a home in the village complete with a porch, a wide entrance, a courtyard, a granary—all constructed with his own labour. He left the courtyard for his mother. In the early days of his marriage, he tried sleeping at home. But the darkness of the four walls and the thatched roof were not for him. He had to see the stars when he opened his eyes. The moon had to shine down on him. He needed to hear the occasional sounds from the cattle shed: a cow clearing its throat, a goat bleating sweetly.

How could he lie around inside the house without any of these? So he made the barnyard his spot again.

He always went back home for dinner. Whenever he felt like being with Ponna, he stayed back after dinner. Whenever he woke up, he went back to the farm. On some nights, he'd go to the barnyard just to sleep. He would come back home as soon as he woke up. All he needed to do was tap on the door gently. Ponna let him in. Initially, it was difficult for Ponna to get used to his habits—this going to and fro between the house and the farm, which was at some distance. She was also scared about the night insects on the farm. But he said, 'For me, night is the real afternoon.'

This was the land in which he was born and raised. This was where he had roamed about. There was no place here that he did not know. Also, Aattur was not a large town where you could easily get lost. What was called the village was just a section of twenty houses. Four or five of those families lived in their fields and used their houses to store their harvest. Beyond that was a section of houses for others. This again had ten or fifteen houses. And a field's length separated one quarter from the other. Kali's field and barnyard were to the east of the village. If he took long strides, he could reach home before he finished chewing a betel nut.

In the afternoons, as soon as he finished his work, he took a nap—in fact, a deep sleep. And he would end up not sleeping well at night. His was a chicken's sleep. If something grated against the fence, the dog would bark and he would wake up. If the chicken started clucking, that was it, he could not sleep any more. So was the case with the calf's moo. And if thoughts of Ponna came to him, he would leave immediately, closing the makeshift gate behind him. Since it was night-time, he would walk in his underwear. He knew which path was safe from stray dogs. Ponna had become used to this too. In the season of toddy, Kali would sleep until the intoxication wore off. Even after that, he would lie awake, shifting about. He had slept very little these past two years.

Kali's mind turned towards an incident some years ago. It was the same Aani month, the time of the chariot festival. His mother-in-law had come to invite them home for the festival. Her home was just the next village, Adaiyur. So she never really stayed the night when she visited them. But that once, surprisingly, she did. And not just that; she dragged her cot to the courtyard next to her daughter's mother-in-law. The two old women whispered to each other all night, but neither he nor Ponna could make out what they were discussing so intently. Only a wall separated them from Ponna, but try as she did, she could not hear anything. Nor could she guess what it could be about. In the ten years that Ponna and Kali had been married, the mothers hadn't spoken so intimately even once. They had their own grievances against each other. Usually they kept their interactions to a minimum. So then what had changed?

'They keep talking back and forth. Maybe they're planning to build a fortress and rule. Or maybe they're scheming against me,' ranted Ponna.

Her suspicion was that they were talking about a second marriage for Kali. Had he too turned against her? She knew that her parents did not mind if Kali were to marry again. But their condition was that he should still keep their daughter with him.

The next morning, she could not keep quiet any longer. She said, 'What, Mother? Looks like you are suddenly getting all intimate with my mother-in-law.' But her mother did not reveal anything.

'We are both old women. What else could we talk about besides the past? Do you think we were scheming to build a castle?'

When her own mother was so reticent about it, there was no way Ponna could have extracted anything from her mother-in-law. She went to Kali bearing her surprise and suspicion.

'I think they have found you a girl. These two hags are trying to ruin my life.'

He said, 'I will marry the girl only if you like her. Don't worry.'

'Oho! You are now entertaining the thought, is it?' she pouted and turned her face away.

Whenever he spoke like that, she was miffed. Then he consoled her. This was a ritual for them. After thinking long and hard about a second marriage, he had abandoned the idea. In truth, the thought had occurred to him once or twice, but his mind simply could not see any other woman in Ponna's place.

eleven

Before he got married, you could find Kali amidst any group of young men just hanging about town. He was also their leader in some ways. But once he got married, Ponna had tied him down somewhat. When the boys teased him, saying, 'Once he saw the girl, he got lost in her,' he quietly walked past them, smiling. But it was true, wasn't it? Ponna's body just dragged him into itself and presented him with whatever he needed. It even gave, volitionally, what he did not ask for, what he did not even know existed. And she had remained the same to him until today. The separation this effected from his male companions was now complete.

In summer, for as long as a month before the temple festival began, crowds started teeming into the town square. Beginning late in the evening and going on till midnight, two drummers would hold forth with their instruments. A temple dance would begin. And as the musicians kept playing the thappu drums, the dance would intensify. Middle-aged men, already well trained in the dance, would go first. Then the novice youth and other boys would join in. Some of the old ones would suddenly decide to show off their expertise. So they would get up and say, 'This is how you do it,' show a few steps, and go back and sit down. They'd yell at the drummers: 'What are you playing? As if someone is dead!' And find fault with the dancers: 'Swing your arms properly!' The others would murmur, 'These old ones never shut up,' and the dancing would continue. Women and children would finish their chores at home and rush to the spot just to see the beauty of the men's hair flapping around their backs and shoulders, their topknots having come undone in all the movement.

Mastering these temple dances was no small matter. The dancers had to internalize the sounds of the drums and dance accordingly. There were over fifty kinds of rhythms, and there were only a few people who were skilled enough to dance to all of them. Those people always danced in the front, and the others danced behind them. Kali was somewhat adept at this dance. He could even follow the dances he didn't really know. For him, there was nothing more joyous than being in the crowd.

On one such occasion, Kali finished his work in a hurry, washed himself and ran to the town square. He did not even have patience to focus on his food, gobbling down what was on his plate before rushing out.

Ponna unleashed her sarcasm. 'What wonder is waiting there for you? Are they waiting for you to inaugurate things? How would this food nourish you if you eat so fast?' But he let nothing bother him.

Her mother-in-law laughed at this: 'He used to roam around like a free ass with his friends. Do you think you can tie him to your lap?' She was delighted that even Ponna could not hold him back from this.

'How can I dance if I eat so much?' he replied. 'Only my belly would go up and down in its fullness.'

There was such delight in dancing in the spacious field in front of the town square! Murugesan from Karumankadu was not very good at dancing. The nuances of the thappu drum simply failed to penetrate his thick head. When everyone took a step in unison, he alone would do something that would make him fall down between their moving feet. Not everyone can dance. And when one comes to terms with this, he can go and sit down with the oldies and watch the others dance. In a way characteristic to spectators, he can also criticize the dancers and pass comments. Failed artistes suddenly become critics. But what do you do about someone who insists on dancing even though he keeps tripping over people's feet? No amount of teasing and taunting deterred Murugesan. With his clumsiness, he sometimes even made other dancers trip over him. He was well built and was the colour of a tender mango shoot.

'Looking at his skin colour, I am a little suspicious,' said Mutthan. 'Maybe we should check with his mother, just in case.' Everyone laughed.

'It should be easy for peasant folk to do this dance,' said Songaan. 'If he can't, it must be some birth defect!' This taunt was followed by more laughter.

Rasu got up, entwined his legs, imitating Murugesan, and said, 'This is real dance.' And more guffaws ensued.

Usually, if the teasing got out of hand, Murugesan would say, 'I will leave you to your dance,' and then move away to join another dance party. But on that day, they had teased him more than he could bear. He was fuming inside. Kali, however, did not know that. He joined in the teasing and said, 'Looks like a doll but moves like a corpse!' Everyone cheered, 'Hear! Hear!'

Murugesan lost it. 'Dey!' he fumed. 'Work is not about this. Work is about *this*,' and he made a lewd gesture, lifting two fingers of his left hand and inserting the index finger of his right hand between them. 'Tell me, now, *who* looks like a doll and works like a corpse?'

Everyone turned to look at Kali. No one laughed but he shrank with shame. He suddenly felt that there was nothing more painful than being in a crowd.

Something else had happened about a year and a half into Kali and Ponna's marriage. People had just started asking about a child. According to them, only the man who induced morning sickness in his wife in the very second month of marriage was a real man. When the girl looked unchanged in over a year and a half, it simply meant the husband's 'work' was not up to the mark. And the entire bunch of Kali's friends had insinuated this several times.

Once, Subramani, who had become a father in the tenth month of his marriage, was in the crowd. When they heard that Muniyannan had made and filtered a fresh batch of arrack, they decided to go there. Muniyannan's arrack was in great demand. There were people who would be flat out for two days on just half a tumbler of his stuff. When they drank together, one of them said, 'Oh, this is great stuff! As vital as water.' And Subramani replied immediately, 'It is not enough if the water you take in is great, the water you send out should be top-class too.'

Everyone glanced at Kali, even if it was for just a moment. Muniyannan's arrack lost its pungency for him that day. He gradually stopped joining this crowd of old friends. He also knew they had nicknamed him 'the impotent one'.

Although he had no children, Kali was very happy with Ponna. He would also ask her now and then to make sure she was happy with him. Her replies always came as intense kisses, and he found peace in that contentment. If the only way to beat this reputation for impotence was to marry again, what would happen if that failed too? Should he ruin the lives of two women? And could Ponna bear his bringing in another woman? She was in the habit of pulling a long face for two days if she saw him even talking to another woman. If he married again, she wouldn't stay. To make things worse, what if the second wife did get pregnant? That would be the end for Ponna. She wanted to believe she was the most important person in his life. Sometimes she even suspected he was fonder of his cattle than he was of her. He tried to reason with her. 'Can this love compare to that?' he said, and buried his face in her bosom. All his heat cooled down.

The moment the thoughts of a second marriage invaded him, all happiness wilted away. It also meant he would need to learn how to handle two women. When his world was already complete with his cattle, his barn and Ponna, could he handle anything more? Also, if the second woman too could not get pregnant, his reputation as an impotent man would be engraved in stone. Thinking through all these things, he abandoned the idea. Whenever someone brought it up, he closed the topic, saying, 'It won't work. Forget it.' They all attributed his hesitation to his fear of Ponna's wrath. 'Well, let them think whatever they want,' he thought. Only he knew that Ponna was scared that he might, at some point, say yes to the idea.

twelve

Uncle Nallayyan too played a role in Kali's refusal to marry again. This was his story: when it came to splitting their inheritance, Uncle Nallayyan's brothers refused to give him his full share.

'Why does a bachelor need the same share as we do?' they all said.

He replied, 'How can you conclude that I will never get married? I might do it even when I am sixty. I won't let any dog touch my food. This is my grandfather's property. Though your father wandered the fields in his underwear, did he add even a handful to it? Tell me!'

The property was divided a year or two after his father's passing. His brothers didn't listen to any of his arguments. They brought along some ten people as mediators, all of whom were on their side. And these men reasoned, 'Why does a single man need so much? Any home is his. Won't the brothers take care of him?

His mother said, 'At least till I am alive I do not want him to have to go to anyone even for a drink of water. Just give us two acres. He and I will live there. After him, it is going to come to you. Isn't it insulting to tell a young and able man that you will feed him? At a time when the oldies are running after women and getting married, he seems to abhor even the scent of a woman.'

Apparently, Uncle had to control his laughter at his mother's naiveté. He said, 'Maybe my mother smelled me for a woman's scent,' and laughed finally. When his brothers realized that their mother was not going to drop his case, they decided to allot two acres to him. But Uncle did not agree with this. He was insistent that he should get his fair share. Men from the community settled matters and asked him, 'Do you agree to this?' He got up, tightened his loincloth and said, 'All right. I agree. Just add one more thing. My brothers seem to have decided that they could just give me a torn cot and some loincloth, throw some food at me and snatch away what is rightfully mine. That's all right. Let it be as they wish. I don't even want the two acres that my mother has asked for. I will let them have all of it. Now, they are giving me this loincloth, right? If this little brother who is inside the loincloth stays quiet and calm, it will all go well. But he does wake up now and then. He'll throw a tantrum for some milk. Just find out and let me know if my sisters-in-law will take care of that.'

He asked all of this with not as much as a smile. His sisters-in-law grew pale in the face and ran inside their houses. The people gathered there murmured to one another as they walked away, 'How can a man talk like this?'

But Uncle called out to them, 'If you are mediators, you should speak for both parties. How can you walk away?'

There were no disputes after that. His share of the inheritance came to him automatically. And his speech became popular in town. The moment someone said, 'Little brother,' the repartee was, 'What? Do you need milk?' It became a code language among young men: 'I've been thirsty for milk, da.' Whenever they saw a loincloth, they were in splits with laughter. They also took to asking Uncle Nallayyan's brothers, 'What did your brother ask for?' and they were amused at how much it angered them.

Uncle did some farming as long as his mother lived. After that, he would sow the land one year, and let it go fallow the next. He also had a farm boy taking care of odd jobs around the field and tending to the cattle. One day, Uncle Nallayyan vanished for a week. When he came back, he had a woman in white with him. The next day onwards, she was working in the fields, dressed in his mother's saris. Uncle, too, worked alongside her happily. The village was overcome with surprise. They said, 'Look at how homebound Nallayyan has become!'

There was no end to the stories of how the two of them would wander about as a couple and make merry. She walked about in new saris and wore lots of flowers in her hair. And he walked along dressed in sparkling white. 'He's become responsible,' everyone thought. But they had a fight one day, and he drove her away. Many people saw her running out of town one evening, wearing the white sari she had first appeared in.

No one knew what went wrong, what the fight was about. His help, the little boy Vediyan, was a sharp one. He was ten or eleven years old and had a lot of freedom around the house. He even cooked for Uncle. If Uncle heard anyone say, 'He eats the food prepared by a his field hand, what kind of a man is he,' he would retort, 'You find a field worker woman fragrant, and only a field hand boy stinks for you?'

Even though a lot of people tried to make Vediyan speak, they could extract nothing out of him. They even tried bribing him with good arrack. He made it look like he was about to spill something, but he never actually divulged anything. They were frustrated: 'Nallayyan has trained this boy well.' When Uncle could get him foreign liquor, why would he fall for this arrack?

Muthu asked Uncle one day when they were lounging about in Kali's barnyard. And it all came out.

'When I bring a dried-up woman home, shouldn't she just shut up and sit around? She started saying she wanted a taali around her neck and a child by me! I got her earrings and this and that and kept her like a queen. But apparently all that was not good enough for her. She wanted a taali. At first I thought the desire would go away soon. But she wouldn't let me touch her without tying a taali round her neck. That's why I hit her, gave her the sari she came in and chased her away.'

They couldn't stop laughing that night. Just to egg him

on some more, Kali said, 'Why, Uncle, couldn't you have let her go in the coloured sari she was wearing?'

'The coloured sari was my mother's. Also, if another woman comes along, I need something to give her, don't I?' he said quietly. 'I can't deal with marriage and all that stuff. It is enough to come and go as I am. As if it's not enough to tie a ring around your nose, they want to tie you to a stalk as well.'

Those words penetrated deep into Kali's mind. He already had a ring around his nose. Should he also tie himself around a stalk now? Since then, whenever someone brought up the topic of a second marriage, Uncle Nallayyan would appear before his eyes.

thirteen

Even though he was curious to find out what his mother and mother-in-law had been discussing, Kali waited for the news to unravel itself. Two nights after his mother-in-law's visit, his mother came to see him in the barnyard. She had raised him single-handedly, working really hard—it was no mean feat farming four acres of land and tending to cattle all by herself. Working alongside her from the time he was a child, Kali took full charge of the place when he was only fourteen or fifteen years old. He was free to do whatever he wanted; he just needed to keep her informed.

He let her be alone and free, just as she desired. She made her own food, and also went to work in other fields. He did not consider that a question of prestige. She wanted to make a little money of her own. What was wrong with that? Let her work as long as she could. If there was something to be done in the field, he told her. She came to help. He paid her what he paid the others, but that was their secret. Wherever she went to work, she simply had to find the time to come and see him every day. Otherwise, she couldn't sleep in peace.

She had very deft hands. In his opinion, no one else could do the things she could. He loved her cooking, but he didn't tell Ponna that. His mother's kootucharu was tasty beyond words. Whenever she planned to make it, she'd tell him in advance, and Ponna wouldn't make any gravy that day. If she steamed groundnuts or other pulses, she would bring it to him in the barn. On all such visits, she would raise the issue of a second marriage. Initially, he refused to participate in the conversation. When she got insistent, his protests grew proportionally stronger. So he thought that a second marriage could not have been the topic of her conversation with his mother-in-law.

It was evident to him that she was struggling to say something. She kept inquiring about the cattle, asking the same things over and over. She spoke about the seeds they were going to sow in the fields that year. Unfortunately, on that particular night, he felt very sleepy. He still had some toddy left in the dried-gourd vessel. He had planned to down it and doze off. But he was not used to drinking in his mother's presence. Though he knew she too was in the habit of drinking, she had never done it in front of him so far. In the toddy season, Muniyannan would keep aside a hanging jarful for her. She would go when it was dark and drink it without anyone coming to know. Even now she was Muniyannan's customer. Whenever he made some, a bottle would be kept aside for her. She would drink a little every day for several days.

Seeing her struggle to begin the conversation, he decided to help her out. After all, the topic was no secret to either of them. 'I have some toddy. Do you want to drink, Amma?' He could not see her face in the dark. Nor could he guess the reason for her silence. Was she cringing that her son had offered her alcohol? Or was her silence to be taken as a yes? He took a small pitcher from under the cot, threw the water out and filled it with toddy and stretched it out to her. When she accepted it, he was happy. He drank what was left in the gourd bowl. He felt that it should now be easier for him to extricate whatever matter was stuck in her throat.

'What, Mother? I am told you and my mother-in-law were conferring all night. Which fortress have you planned to capture?' he prodded.

He could see that her pitcher was not yet empty. She was the kind who drank slowly. He was getting to know that now.

'What fortress are we going to capture at this age? If we die today, we are fully gone tomorrow. What else would we talk about? It was about you two.'

'What? Talking about a second marriage again?'

'You have said no to it several times. Ponna's parents are fine with the idea. If we are a little forceful, even Ponna would say yes. But you refuse. I don't understand why. Anyway, drop it.'

His mother spoke gently and at a measured pace that day, although it was in her nature to shout. She appeared completely new to him. Even when you have spent years with some people, their real faces are revealed only when the right time comes. God knows how many faces lie concealed forever, with no opportunity to reveal themselves.

His mother spoke without a break. Perhaps she was afraid that if she paused, she might not be able to resume speaking. 'You have done all the prayers you could do,' she intoned. 'You have even walked around the barren rock that one in a thousand people take on. Nothing has happened. Whether we have children or not, we are all going to die one day; we don't live forever. When we are alive, we should be useful to the people around us. What else is left for human beings? Your father died leaving me all alone. But my plight would have been so much harder if I did not have you. I had my son entwined around my legs, and so I could bear all my difficulties happily. You were the only hold I had in life. Don't you need one such for yourself? When people ask "Do you have grandchildren?" I am unable to reply. I wonder why this earth doesn't split into two and swallow me whole. If this is how hard it is for me, it must be so much more for you and Ponna. The wretched people around us do not see what a man has. They only see what he does not have. We have to hold our heads high in front of these people, my son. Please don't get me wrong. This is not something a mother should talk about with her son. But I have dared to speak. Please listen.'

He truly could not understand what she was leading up to. He could hear her gulp down the toddy left in her pitcher. He still had some left in the gourd bowl. She might need more. When she put her pitcher down, he said, 'Do you want more, Amma?'

She declined and proceeded to say, 'Karattaiyan and Devatha of Karattur have so many ways of helping people.

From the moment the flag is hoisted to when the gods come down and go back up the hill, how many miracles they perform for how many people! People in my father's house are entitled to carry the deities. And they have been doing so till date. I was born in that family. Will the gods fail to show me a way? We roamed around that street from the beginning to the end of the festival. The eighth day, when the gods come down, and the eighteenth day, when they go back up the hill, are very important. But since I attained puberty, I have not attended the event of the eighteenth day. They wouldn't send me. You know why. You have gone for it with and without my knowledge. This year, we need to send Ponna there. And you must agree to this.'

Kali was speechless. He had never thought there could be such a motive for attending the eighteenth day of the festival. Which man would say yes to such a thing? His mind went blank, and whatever his mother said after that was dwindling into mere noise.

'Who is without lack in this world? The gods have made sure everyone lacks something or the other. But the same god has also given us ways to fill that lack. We don't know whether the problem is with you or her. But we know there is a problem, and there is a way out of it. Why don't we give it a try? If you accept it, it will all work out. A lot of women go this and that way. Who knows about these things? Even if people know, they ignore it. They say nothing is wrong as long as it is done in secret. This will be done in secret, too, but only with your permission. She is yours, after all.'

He saw a world of utter silence in front of him. In the dark, he could sense the movement of her lips.

'All men who set their foot in Karattur on the eighteenth day are gods. It is god who is giving this. It is not a problem if we keep our mind on god. Who knows which god comes with what face? It is the nature of gods not to reveal their faces. If you say yes, we can go to this year's festival. Well, we don't have to go from here. Ponna's mother can take her. You don't have to go along. You can be here or in your father-in-law's place. It is your choice. Think about it and let me know. Everything is in your hands now, my little god.'

He did not know when his mother left. He also did not know how long he had been sitting there. His eyes were wide open. Usually, he fed the cows once at midnight, but tonight he could not even hear their mooing. Amma, why did you struggle so hard to bring me up? Just so you could push me into this terrible fire? You could have killed me even before I came into this world.

His eyes were bloodshot in the morning. And they stayed so forever after that.

fourteen

For the people of Karattur, the chariot festival was a three-month affair. The preparations began as soon as the month of Aani started. And the shops and stalls lasted till the month of Aadi. But, strictly speaking, the festival itself was only for eighteen days. For a lot of people the nineteenth day was the day of completion. So if you include that as well, it was a nineteen-day-long festival. The deities that were brought down from the hill on the eighth day returned uphill on the eighteenth day. On those two nights, crowds poured in to get a vision of the gods. And more than the day the gods came down, it was the day of their return that was charged and climactic.

Crowds would gather from the morning onwards. They would erect water pandals on all sides to dispense drinking water to the travellers. The fields would lie untended. Even if there had been good rains, they would stop with the first ploughing of the topsoil. All the carts bringing people to the festival would be parked in these fields. It would look like a fair for bullock carts! People also brought large parcels of food. But they could buy food from the several stalls too. There was no dearth of cultural performances in the four main streets or in the pillared temple halls at the foothills.

At the peak of the celebration, all rules were relaxed. The night bore witness to that. Any consenting man and woman could have sex. Bodies would lie casually intertwined. Darkness cast a mask on every face. It is in such revelry that the primal being in man surfaces.

No one sent unmarried women to the festival. But women over thirty were to be seen everywhere. Young men roamed all over the place.

Kali too went there in the days before his marriage. He started roaming the streets when the evening set in. That night there was no business in the devadasis' street. Those women dressed themselves up to dance in the temple halls. They laughed as they went about: 'Who is going to look at us today?'

In that first year, when his body was ready to get to know a woman's, he was overcome with shyness and he escaped from all the women and hid under a bullock cart. Lying there, he saw all the movements in the dark around him. He didn't dare to come out. On their way back home the next day, Muthu teased him. He gestured the number two to Kali, who was frustrated that he had let the opportunity slip by. He would now have to wait another year. But Muthu made sure Kali did not have to wait a whole year. By the following year's festival, Kali had gained enough experience.

Kali did not know that this was a special day for women who did not have children. He could not bring himself to agree to send Ponna there. Nor did he tell her anything about it. But he told her this much: that they were not going to her place for the festival that year. Usually, that period was a break for her, and she would go and spend a week at her mother's place. During that time, she would also go in a bullock cart to see the festival. In fact, the two of them definitely went on at least one of the three days when the large chariot was out. Seeing her shrunken and disappointed face, he took her there himself. He bought her all she wanted from the shops there.

But that time, all he said to her was, 'It has been ten years since we got married. Why do we still need to go there for the festival? Let's do it here this time.' She did not protest, but she sensed that something was wrong. They did not go even when her mother came and invited them to the last day of the festival. Instead, they went to the large snake pit in the fields and offered a rooster for prayer. When he poured the kuzhambu for his mother, she did not meet his eyes. As far as he was concerned, that year's ordeal was over. The worry could wait another year.

He was still confused whether to bring this up with Ponna or not. He thought she would refuse. In fact, he hoped that that's what she would do. But he was too scared to broach the subject with her. One moment, he felt the courage to start the conversation, but as soon as he looked at her, he hesitated, feeling completely tongue-tied. At other times, he felt very certain that he should not talk to her about this at all. But she might ask for a reason if next year too he said no to going to her mother's place for the festival. He knew he could not keep it from her forever, but he was also unsure whether he should ask for her opinion about this or declare his decision.

Her body had entwined with his for ten years now. It had met his fragrances for ten years now. He felt that every bit of her body was his and his alone. If another fragrance were laid over it, it would be a blemish. And he told himself with certainty that once it was blemished, he wouldn't touch it. If all men were gods, then let the god take possession of Kali's body too.

He trusted her. He recalled the time when the young men of the village had started teasing him for not having a child even after two years of marriage. Presuming that they knew everyone's secret in the village, they concluded that Kali was a useless fellow. All their sympathies started flowing towards Ponna. They thought they could lure her if they put some effort into it. He heard that they had placed bets on it. Karuppannan, who owned a palm grove, was the mastermind of this scheme. He had a fair complexion and was under the delusion that women would just fall all over him for the colour of his skin. He was married and had children. It was his wife who did all the work at home and in the fields. All he did was sit around in the town square, playing dice and ogling women. He also waxed eloquent about his exploits. But most of them actually turned out to be wishful thinking.

He got into the bizarre habit of intercepting Ponna when she went alone to the fields, and grinning at her ingratiatingly. He even started coming to Kali's house in the middle of the day with his friends to play dice. Ponna became his waitress, bringing him water, matchbox, and so on. Kali would come back from the barnyard in the middle of the night and knock on the door. But Ponna was not sure any more that it could only be Kali. Fearing gossip, she decided to spend one night in the barnyard. Holding him in her embrace, she poured her heart out. His chest, wet with her tears, heaved in anger.

'Isn't it because I have no children that people look at me this way?' she cried. 'If I had that blessing, would I have to suffer this disgrace? Every dog thinks I am just a stone standing at the street corner that it can rub itself against.'

The next day, Kali encountered Karuppannan. As usual, the latter's talk was loaded with innuendoes.

'Kali, my brother, you have two coconut trees. Can't you water them properly? Look at the new blossoms. They are dried and shrivelled up.'

Kali decided there was no point in beating around the bush. He charged in head-on.

'Karuppannan, you have no idea how I go about watering things. Haven't you married off your sister Racchi to someone in Pazhavur? Ask her, she will tell you! Why do you think she keeps coming back here? Do you think she comes to see you, her brother? You poor thing! Your wife is lamenting to everyone that you are jobless and sitting around the town square. Ask her and find out what job you are good for. Don't worry about my coconut trees. Keep your game of dice to the town square.'

A dark shadow fell over Karuppannan's face. Though Kali had mixed a good deal of lies with the truth, the conviction with which he spoke rattled Karuppannan and chased him away from the square. He tightened his loincloth and changed his haunt to a shaded spot in the field. After this, Ponna did not have to speak to any random man. If she had to, she hurled words that stung like an ant in the crotch. Her circle grew smaller. She stayed away from people, and kept them away.

Kali was absolutely sure that Ponna would not agree to go to the eighteenth day of the festival.

fifteen

Nallayyan's arrival at the barnyard that day was like a balm to Kali's aching heart. Kali had not seen him for a week. Perhaps he had gone on one of his spontaneous trips.

'What, Chittappa? You vanished for so long,' Kali said to him.

'Oh, I was very much in town. The farm boy and I together thought we could turn our barnyard to look just like yours. Hence there was a lot of work to do.'

'What kind of work?'

'We had been just pushing aside all the cow dung to one side, and it had collected into a mound. We carried it all out. Then we wiped the floor clean. Then we killed a chicken and ate well.'

'Has it turned into a good-looking barnyard?' Kali asked.

'You manage to stay put in this place like a rock. I can't work like that. If I feel like it, I spend the whole week in the market. Then I suddenly remember I was actually born a farmer. That's how it goes.'

'But, Uncle, why would you spend the entire week in the market?'

'Well, I go to the Eeriyur market on Monday, Karattur market on Tuesday, then to the Wednesday market, and so on. You too should try going to these places. That's when you will get a sense of how the world works. Where do you think I found that white-saried woman? It was in our own Tuesday market.'

'How does it work, Uncle?'

'Just like there are men who deal in cattle, there are men for this too. I asked one of them if he could send the woman in the white sari to me for a month. He checked with her. We agreed on food and clothes for her and also twenty-five rupees in hand. I gave him five rupees. Everything went well. But that whore was not content with just a man in her life. She needed a husband.'

'But if you had married her and had children, it could've helped you with your property. You would also be able to hold your head high in the village. Don't you agree, Uncle?'

'Why? For whom do I hang my head low now? It is only you who is relentlessly talking about having children. All right, go ahead and have a child. But do you know how you should live? Like that crow that has built a nest on that palm tree. When it knows it is going to lay eggs, it builds its nest. Then it incubates the eggs and hatches them. It finds food for the little ones and takes care of them until they grow their own wings. Once that happens, what do you think is the relationship between the baby crow and its mother? They go their separate ways. "You got your wings, now get out of here, and fend for yourself." That's the way to live. Instead, we give birth, raise them, get them married, save money and struggle. Is this any way to live? If we were more like crows and cuckoos, I'd also like to have children.'

He followed that up with many other things. But nothing registered in Kali's mind. What he had said had told him that he needn't care what the village said, that he didn't need a child. After all, Uncle didn't give a hoot what anyone thought, and he wanted for nothing. How happy he was! He was the first one to introduce soap to the village. When he bathed with soap, the entire well smelled wonderful. When he travelled out of town, he wore a lovely tunic. He had cut off his topknot long ago. If one was constantly worried about not having a child, could one be this happy? These people are asking me to send my wife to another man just for the sake of a child. What if I decide I don't need a child at all?

If you are always worried about what others are going to say, you will always be in trouble. When Nallayyan cropped off his head-knot and came back into town, it created such a ruckus. They held a community meeting and condemned him. Everyone spoke against him. They argued that now that someone had dared to do away with his topknot, it wouldn't rain any more in the village; that no one would want to stay within bounds any more. They ruled that he should not fetch water from the common well, that workers should not go to his house, no one in the village should speak to him, and no one should accept money from him for the temple festivals. Some people even opined that they should shave his head completely, put red and black marks on him and parade him around the village in punishment.

Finally, the village head called Nallayyan aside and said, 'Just own up to your mistake. Tell them you will grow the hair again. We will just fine you and let you go.'

But Uncle wouldn't budge. 'If the village's honour resides in my bloody hair, I will grow it,' he said. 'I don't even mind growing a beard and a moustache. I will grow them and sit around like you all, plucking lice from it. But add another thing to it. It was only yesterday that I shaved off my pubic hair, because it was itching too much. Now if your village's honour is also dependent on my pubic hair, let me know right away. I will grow that too.'

The crowd roared in laughter at Nallayyan's speech. The village head and the others did not know what to say. As they dispersed they said, 'Is he even a farmer? Why did we even think of dropping all our work and getting together to discuss this? Let's just think of him as a lunatic walking around in our village. From now on, don't bring any of his matters to the council.'

Uncle said, 'In all the big towns, people have done away with these long topknots a long time ago. It is only you who are combing it for lice even now. Why should I subject myself to that?' and he roamed around with his cropped hair.

Kali had often thought that he lacked his uncle's courage. He was fuming on the inside at his inability to communicate his decision on the matter of sending Ponna to the festival. He decided that he should find an opportunity to tell Ponna very firmly that he did not want children. It was much better than losing one's honour. And he also wanted to know what was on her mind.

Her plan was to somehow make him accept the previous year's invite to the chariot festival from her parents. When she brought it up gently, he realized he couldn't delay it any more.

'Do you remember how your mother and mine were whispering all night to each other last year when she had come to invite us? Do you know what they were talking about?'

She had been curious about it then. But when nothing unravelled for over a week, she had concluded it must have been something to do with old age and their reminiscences of the past. She even forgot about it. Now when she realized he had known about it for a year and had kept it from her, she was angry.

'I didn't tell you only because I wasn't sure how you would take it,' he started and told her about the fourteenth day of the festival when the gods returned to the hill. She didn't know about it. He was surprised that this open secret had still not spread like wildfire.

'Ah! You and my brother used to be delighted to go see the gods. I now realize what it was all about,' she snapped.

'No! We truly went to see the gods. Why are you accusing us now?' he said.

In his mind, he was looking for words to console her. She seemed to fill the darkness of the barnyard. He embraced her from behind. This was the embrace that cured him of all worries. He murmured into her ear.

'Don't you know I hung around with your brother only to get to you? Would these eyes that had had a taste of you even look at another woman? Even when I was fourteen or fifteen, I decided you were mine. And it has stayed that way,' he pleaded and buried his face in her neck. But he could not tell if her anger was gone. Then, still in his arms, she turned to face him. He felt emboldened by her hand gently caressing his back.

'Will you listen to your mother and mine and go on the day when the gods retreat?' he continued. His heart was thumping, waiting for her reply.

She murmured: 'If you want me to go for the sake of this wretched child, I will.'

His hold around her relaxed. This was not the answer he had expected.

He moved away from her. For a moment he wondered if this was her way of getting back at him for his exploits before their marriage. He lay on the cot facing the sky. She realized that she had failed to give him the reply he had wanted to hear. She rushed to him in panic and spread herself upon him. Laying her head against his cheek, she looked for words of consolation. After all, the core of this relationship consisted in using consoling words.

'Maama,' she said, melting, 'I thought you wanted me to, for the sake of a child. Will I ever do anything you do not like? You are everything to me. Despite everyone's pressuring you for a second marriage, you have said no to it. That's why I said I would do what you want me to do. Please don't be angry . . .'

But the sex they had that night was the worst they had ever had.

sixteen

He did not say anything about going to her parents' place. Nor did she bring it up again. But they made peace enough to go together to watch the chariot.

It looked like things were back to normal. She felt her response to him had been terribly wrong. Was it her desperation that she should have a child by any means that had led her to say what she did? Did it even sound like he wanted her to? She had failed to see that he was merely testing the waters. Usually, it was not difficult for her to say exactly what he wanted to hear. After all, she had been doing it all these years. But she blundered on that one day. Anger had clouded her eyes.

But then again, what was so terrible about what she had said? All she had implied was that if *he* was fine with the idea, she didn't mind. She genuinely thought it was a way out of being insulted and ridiculed by everyone. Didn't he remember the humiliation they suffered at the puberty ceremony of Chellama's daughter's? Chellama was like an older sister to him. So, as an uncle to her daughter, there was no way he could not have gone for the ceremony. She invited them lovingly. By then, Ponna had stopped going anywhere, but Kali insisted that she accompany him.

Her mother-in-law kept ranting, 'How can a man go alone and stand in a girl's puberty ceremony? Don't you have any brains? The girl is the granddaughter of our close relatives. And how can an uncle's wife not go to the function? When I am dead and gone, don't you want some people to still keep some contact, visit now and then? Or do you think you would send me away and be done with it?'

Unable to bear all this, Ponna went along. There were nine plates of gifts at the ceremony. Ponna carried one of these plates in the procession. It was only later that she came to know that they had grudgingly given her a plate to carry, because it was the convention for the uncles' wives to do so. There was also a custom meant to ward off the evil eye, wherein all the aunts were called to spin red balls of rice in a large circle around the girl's body and then toss them away. Ponna was standing to a side with Kali. He nudged her to go forward to be part of that ritual. Another woman had also said, 'If you are her uncle's wife, you too should do it.'

But when she tucked in her pallu and went forward, Chellama's brother's wife dragged her aside and said, 'You stay away.' If a childless woman did the ritual, would it make the girl barren? Was she that inauspicious? She pulled Kali by the arm and brought him outside. While he kept imploring, 'Let it go, let it go,' she kept walking in the dark. And he ran after her.

Didn't he take that insult personally? Even for death ceremonies in the village, no one asked him to fetch water in the cremation ground. If a child is so important to establish oneself as a human being in this world, why shouldn't she dare to do what it takes to accomplish that? After all, she was not the kind who went in secret and slept with other men in the fields, was she? All she said was that if he approved, she was fine with the idea. What could she do if that upset him? As the last day of the festival approached, her mother-in-law started giving her meaningful glances. It looked like if Ponna nodded just a little, her mother-in-law would herself take her to the festival. If it was a lazy, adamant bull, you could make it budge by biting its tail. You could shock it into action by staging a little fire. But what could she do with this obstinate man?

The humiliations she had had to suffer because of this one problem were endless. She could not even go to their own fields during the sowing season for fear that others would broach the topic. So she would lock herself inside the house. Couldn't he understand these things? He responded to the moment by cajoling and consoling her, and then forgot all about it the very next minute.

In the months of Aani or Aadi, depending on when the rains arrived, they would sow groundnuts. There was only one plough to each field. And it took two or three days to plough a field with one. It could get tiresome. But if four or five of them got together to work on each field, not only was it fun, they could also finish ploughing each field in a day. Sometimes, they would even take five ploughs at once to a field and be done in half a day. They first ploughed those fields which had loose topsoil that didn't hold water for long. Next, it was the elevated fields with red soil. Low-lying ones were ploughed last. The order of preference was based on the soil and its moisture content. Women went to sprinkle manure water in the ploughed furrow and to lift and give seed baskets to the men.

Then one year, something happened. That year too, they ploughed in a specific order, working together in everyone's fields. On the last day, they focused on Vellivel's field. He was from Thidamankaadu. There had been no rain for five days, not even a drop. So the land was not very wet. They reasoned that it was all right if it was not wet on top. As long as the soil was wet underneath, there was no big problem. So, they went ahead and sowed the seeds. On that day, Ponna helped by lifting the baskets of seeds. Originally, her task had been to sprinkle seed-water, but Vellivel's wife, Karuvachi, who was supposed to do it, came down with severe leg pain and couldn't be part of the work. Sprinkling only involved walking behind whoever ploughed. But lifting the seed baskets also involved running back and forth. The seeds were all kept amassed in one corner of the field. They would have to keep replenishing the baskets with the seeds and be ready. The moment the sprinklers signalled, the lifters would have to run carrying the baskets. If any one of them delayed, even for a bit, it would halt the work of all five ploughs. Also, they had to walk along with the sprinklers and drop the seeds evenly. Ponna had to do all these tasks that day. Her legs were exhausted from all the running. She could sleep only after she massaged them with some hot water. But what came of all that suffering?

The following year, they did not include Kali in their sowing team. He worked alone in his field and Ponna did the sprinkling. They didn't know the reason. Then they heard that Vellivel did not get a good yield the year before, and whatever he got was of poor quality.

Someone had said, 'That barren woman ran up and down carrying seeds. How do you expect them to grow once she has touched them?'

They never found out who said it. Everyone kept pointing to someone else. They could not even find out if it was a man who said it or a woman. But this much was clear: everyone seemed to agree with it. Ponna's father and brother had always asked her to fill and carry the seed baskets whenever they had sowed. Their yield had never suffered because of this. After marrying Kali, it was she who did those tasks in the field. Only when they needed extra help did Kali hire someone. And nothing went wrong.

Ponna confronted Vellivel's wife on the way and gave her a piece of her mind: 'You said you were in severe leg pain and begged me to go. That's why I carried the seeds. Do you think I am obliged to go and work in your field? I might be barren, but nothing I have touched has ever withered. The plant I planted is flowering now, the tree I planted is bearing fruit, the calf I brought has grown and birthed many of its own, and the egg that I helped incubate has hatched a beautiful chick . . . There is nothing I have touched that has not flourished. Anything sowed in a dry land will go waste, no matter who helps in carrying the seeds. If you—wife and husband—had taken better care of the land, maybe it would have all grown.'

The next year, Ponna refused to work even in their own field. But Kali placated her and took her along. Since then, they worked with one plough. And if he didn't learn his lesson even after everyone had cast him away, what could she do?

seventeen

Though Kali had resumed normal conversation with Ponna, he was constantly haunted by her words.

He was now convinced that women were terrible creatures. Mother tells the son, 'Send your wife to another man.' The other mother is ready to take her own daughter to it. And Ponna says, 'I will, if you are fine with it.' No one seemed to have even an iota of hesitation anywhere. He, on the other hand, was still hesitant to talk about those long-gone days when he had been to the festival. While a man felt so shy about these matters, look at these women! What they dared to do! If someone told them that the only way to have a child was to drop a rock on his head while he slept, would Ponna be ready to do that too?

These thoughts drained his trust in her. A falseness entered in his sweet words to her. His embrace was no longer whole-hearted. There was no softness when he made love to her, not the usual generosity that let him include her in its sway. He came to be possessed by a fury for revenge, a desire to pound her violently and tear her apart. It was hot in the barnyard those days, even at night. He'd wake up suddenly and go home. Ponna kept the earthen wick lamp burning softly through the night. He would peep through the gaps in the wooden planks on the door to see if she was asleep. Sometimes he even went back to the barnyard without waking her up. Whenever he saw that the light inside was put out, that there was nothing but darkness, he panicked. On such days, he listened carefully for any sound that came from inside the house. Sometimes, his tapping on the door woke his mother. When she asked, 'Who is it?' he replied shyly, 'It's just me. Go back to sleep.'

A sense of urgency and carelessness started pervading all his actions. However much she tried to hold him tight and take him inside her, all he wanted was to hold back adamantly and ejaculate as soon as he could. Whenever he decided to drink loads of arrack, which he knew would knock him out till morning, he asked her to come and stay in the barn. He would force her to drink. Earlier, on the nights he drank, his body lost its harshness and spread on her like a fluid. He would chatter happily for a long time. On such nights, he wore only the loincloth. She'd playfully pull it open. But he would feel no shame. She would say in mock anger, 'You have no shame. Look at you! Sitting with nothing on.' And he'd reply, 'Why should I feel any shame in front of you? Why don't you be naked too?' But there was none of that intimacy now.

Now he downed the arrack like water in quick gulps and passed out right away. At whatever time he came to at night, he jumped on her and took control of her. It took him several mornings to regain a sense of balance. 'The drinking is getting out of control, maama. Please drink less,' she said lovingly. He responded with a slight smile. His face never blossomed again in a full smile.

Whenever he crushed her underneath him, she begged, 'Maama, please don't show your anger on me this way. It is unbearable. Just hit me. Get a club and beat me to pulp if you want. But please don't torture me like this.' His heart went out to her. His embrace and kisses then said to her, 'It was my mistake, dear.'

When she menstruated every month, she came to sit and cry in the barn. It was consoling to bury her face in his lap. He'd ruffle her hair and say, 'Let it go. We should be used to it by now.' But she kept hoping things would change. Sometimes, her crying made him cry too. So they cried together, lamenting their fate. Ironically, it made him happy on the inside whenever she got her periods on time and came crying to him. The way his mind worked, she was trustworthy as long as she was menstruating regularly.

Subsequently, he reasoned: 'Poor thing. How can I be so suspicious because of just that one thing she said? She only said it in the urge to do something to have a child of her own. Does that mean I can conclude she would go with any man? Didn't she come to me complaining about Karuppannan's advances? She said what she said because of me—she said it for me. She said, "I will go if you ask me to." And I didn't ask her to. Then why would she go?' This made him treat her with affection, and it looked as though the Kali she knew was back.

But it lasted only a week. He then got back to being irritable, and she was at a loss for words to placate him. But since she was annoyed too, it was easy for her to raise her voice. It put him in place a little if she shouted at him. He never raised his voice. Even when he had to call out to her from the field, he didn't yell. He'd move closer and call her in a voice that sounded like he had a raven hidden deep inside his throat. She felt bad that she needed to shout and fight with him. This went on for a year. She had no other way but to observe him closely and choose her responses accordingly.

eighteen

Then came the year when Muthu came in person to invite them for the chariot festival. He was determined to somehow convince his sister and Kali to go. He came on the eve of the procession of the big chariot and spoke to his sister first. Her face was clouded in sadness. She wanted to visit her home, but how could she go without Kali's permission?

'I will speak to Kali,' he said to her. 'You should be ready to leave with me in the morning. Let Kali come a few days from now.'

Muthu and Kali had known each other since childhood. Sometimes Muthu came here and stayed for a few days. Even Kali's mother thought he would listen to whatever Muthu said.

'Ponna, please go to the eighteenth day of the festival this year,' said her mother-in-law to her happily. 'Your brother will take care of everything. How long can we keep looking at each other's faces in this house? Don't we want a child to bounce around in this place? We have a lovely home. Don't we need a child to crawl around all this space? Everything will go well. Be ready to leave tomorrow.'

Ponna, however, felt certain that Kali wouldn't say yes. Even if he relented and agreed to send her to her village, he would definitely not say yes to her going to the eighteenth day of the festival. He was still smarting at what she had said a year ago. Why would he change his mind now? Muthu left for the barn, asking Ponna to bring dinner there.

Fencing it around with dried, thorny twigs, Kali had kept his barnyard very well. The fence, which sagged nowhere, was strewn with creepers here and there. The thatched roof was stitched close and tight. A bullock cart could easily go in and come out. And then, of course, there was the portia tree. It had spread, arresting time in its branches. In its shade were tethered two bulls and a cow. There was a calf bull with a bite-guard in its mouth; its legs were tied. All of them somehow fit under the shade of the tree. When it started drizzling, Kali would take the calf alone inside the shed. Under the dense foliage of the tree, the rain sprinkled in gentle droplets. There was a large rectangular waste pit in one corner.

On the other side of the portia tree was the enclosure for goats. There weren't too many of them, however. Just two nanny-goats; one of them had four kids. And looking at them, you could say how full of milk the goat was. The other goat was pregnant, its tummy bulging. There were also two sheep wandering about untethered. The little hut inside the enclosure was meant to keep the goats from the rain. Next to the enclosure were stacks of harvested groundnuts and corn. The latter in particular looked abundant and robust. It would last for a year even if the rains failed. There was not a speck of dirt on the cemented thrash floor. It was kept very clean. Beyond that was the shed with its thatched roof looking like the half-spread wings of a bird. Of the two cots that were inside this shed, one was stood upright. On the other side of the shed was an empty space of about a square metre. Bordering the fence were a neem tree, a vadanarayana tree and two palm trees. It had been two years since the palm fronds were pruned. By the dried bird shit that was all over them, you could tell that the chickens were in the habit of climbing on to the palm tree. Muthu was delighted to roam around the barn. Kali was always thoughtful in whatever he did.

During one of his earlier visits here, Muthu saw two hens wandering around with a large group of chickens. There must have been over twenty chickens for each of them. If they grew up, one could start a poultry farm. But it was a nuisance to keep too many hens. They would get into the cow dung kept to a side and spread it all over the flat floor. That was why Kali was in the habit of gathering the cow dung from the floor well before the chickens got down from the tree. And only after throwing some kambu millet in front of the shed would he even let the little chicks out of the large hay basket.

Once the chicks got bigger, there was a chicken feast every week. Whenever someone came to visit, he would catch hold of a chicken. If he decided to go to the Tuesday market, he could probably sell them very easily, but he was reluctant to do that. Sengannan, the chicken seller, came now and then to buy them for a decent price. After all, he needed to make a profit of at least four or eight annas per chicken. Muthu was amazed at how well the fowls looked.

If you let the hen out of the coop after it hatched ten or fifteen little chicks, then in a month all you were left with were four or five of them. That's because crows bothered them incessantly. Eagles too. Even when the chicks grew bigger, they could not escape the claws of the large kite. It would lie concealed in the dense foliage of a tree and attack suddenly. Whenever it swooped down, it always left with a chicken held tight in its beak. It was almost impossible to save the chicken from them. But then how did Kali manage to keep so many of them alive?

With a smile, Kali pointed to the two palm trees at the back of the shed.

'What do these unpruned palm fronds have to do with the chicken?' Muthu asked.

'Look carefully, machan. Keep looking at the tree. You will get it in a little while.'

He never explained anything. He only drew your attention to things. Muthu kept staring at the trees. Two blackbirds took turns visiting the tree. Was Kali keeping the palm fronds intact for these birds?

'It is not enough if you find little caves and crevices to hide in. You also need some brains. But how can I expect that from you!' Kali teased. Then he explained.

The blackbird built its nest only on palm trees with dense fronds. From the time it begins to build the nest to the time it lays its eggs, incubates them, and nourishes the little ones, no other bird can come near the tree. The male and female blackbirds would take turns guarding the nest. If another bird approached the tree, they would peck at it and chase it away. These birds might be small and fit into the palm of one's hand, but they were courageous. They could even daringly chase away an eagle. And if you let the chicks out during this time when the blackbirds were nesting on the tree, the chicks would be safe. In this way, the blackbirds guarded the little chicks too.

This was how it worked. The moment Kali noticed the blackbirds surveying the palm trees, he prepared the hen coop. There were always one or two hens laying eggs. But if those eggs were not enough, he bought at least twenty eggs from someone and placed them in the coop. For this reason alone, he never cut the palm fronds. He only cleared away, once every two years, the dried ones that hung from the tree.

Ponna always cried, 'You take such good care of these little chickens. And I am unable to lay a little one in your hands.'

Muthu was truly amazed at how well kept Kali's barn was. He went around expressing his wonder to everyone.

A lot of people tried to keep a barn like Kali's, but they couldn't sustain the work. Nor did they have the patience. What did they think? That if they did not prune the palm fronds, the blackbird will somehow land up on its own? The place also needed to be a safe one for the birds, like Kali's barn was. In this respect, the blackbirds were far more intelligent than human beings.

It was Kali who had built the barnyard. His mother was concerned that land spread over more than half an acre was getting wasted. It was a disorganized space, with the harvest piled up on one side and the flat thrash floor on the other. He brought them closer, planned the space, and insisted that a barnyard was essential for farmers. He thought of it in such a way that the portia, which had already been planted, became the front side of the barn. Muthu, who was assisting Kali then, said, 'It would be nice to have the shed as soon as you enter.' But Kali felt that it was important to see the cows' faces while entering. He also felt that this way, by walking past the cows every day, it would be easier to assess if the thrash floor needed cleaning. So he put the shed at the back.

Muthu now recollected the days he had spent in this space with Kali. What happy times they were! If they finished their work in the fields and attended to the cattle on time, no one bothered them for anything. They were like the temple bull that roamed around freely. After his marriage, Kali was worried about a child. Muthu's parents too spoke about it all the time. They even told him with conviction, 'It is too late for a child now. That's it. Your machan and you have been great friends for a long time now. Then what? It is to your children that he is going to leave all he has.'

Muthu did not care for the property. He felt that Kali's life would gain some normalcy if he had a child. The Kali he knew before he married Ponna was a different man. Laughter and revelry were his natural states of being. The moment he heard that there was a theatre performance happening ten villages away, he'd gather a crowd and go there. If someone told him that there was a good movie running at Kannan Talkies in Karattur, he would go. The first time Muthu watched a film, he was very confused. Were those people dancing for real in front of him or were they dolls? There were forests, houses, palaces and songs. Where did they all come from? Kali pointed to the projector room at the back. Muthu was wonderstruck at how all of that was coming through a little hole in the wall. The film operator there was an acquaintance of Kali's. They smoked together sometimes. There were a number of things Kali used to do. Now he confined himself to the barnyard.

The cattle and the portia were all that he needed. Muthu felt he could not leave Kali to this lifestyle. He needed to be dragged out of this. And having a child could do it. So, even if this was the last resort, Muthu was determined he should somehow send Ponna to the eighteenth day of the festival that year. He did not know how to broach this topic with Kali. But he had to. Also, whether he spoke to Kali or not, and whether Kali gave his permission or not, he had to make sure Ponna went to see the gods. Muthu was certain of that.

nineteen

When Muthu entered the barnyard, Kali was feeding the cows. 'I am staying here tonight, mapillai!' Muthu shouted out to him. It felt like the entire barnyard was trying to contain a great excitement within it. There was joy on Kali's face too. At the thought of a night in the barnyard with his old friend, a celebratory mood pervaded his mind.

'Machan, does toddy suffice, or do you want arrack?' he asked Muthu.

'After drinking toddy every day now, it has lost its zing for me, mapillai. See if you can get some sharp arrack.'

'All right. I'll be back,' said Kali, and took the ochre dhoti that was hanging on the hook, tied it over his loincloth, and left. 'Shall I also kill a chicken?' he asked.

Muthu replied, 'Have you forgotten the rules of the fast? We can do all that on the last day of the festival. Not today. I have asked Ponna to bring dinner here. She will bring something soon. Don't worry.'

Kali closed the thatched gate behind him and blended with the darkness outside. Muthu knew he would bring some good arrack. The moment the temple flag was hoisted in Karattur and the festival was on, you couldn't as much as smell a fish. That was how strictly the rules of the fast had to be followed. The strictures were relaxed once the gods returned to the hill. There would be no dearth of cows, goats and pigs. Also, rows of bullock carts carrying baskets of fish would start streaming into town.

When they were little boys, they went together to herd cattle. There was a rugged stretch of land between the two villages. It was as high as two coconut trees and was as wide as the living quarters of the village. People called it Narikkaradu, the Fox Land. In the main cultivation season, that was the grazing ground for cattle. In what looked like something arranged out of large rocks, there were plenty of short trees and bushes. What started as time spent together tending to the flock developed into a friendship. They roamed around together, and they had nothing to hide from each other. Once the festival started, they wandered about the streets of the town every other day for months. They could walk and sprint the eight-mile distance in half an hour. Not that they needed to get there in any hurry. In the months of Chithirai and Vaigasi, they would sit in the front yards of different houses and flirt with the girls. Once they were done taking care of the cattle, what was left for these young men to do?

It was also quite common for them to stay in each other's houses. Strictly speaking, their relationship was that of an uncle and a nephew. But they addressed each other in the

friendliest of terms, as 'vaada' and 'poda'. Whenever Kali
went to Muthu's house, he had an eye on Ponna. It was a
wonder for him to have seen her as a child and then to see
her suddenly blossoming into a girl. As soon as he turned
eighteen, his mother started looking for a bride for him.
Since Kali knew that Muthu was privy to everything about
him, he was not sure how to walk up to him and say, 'Give
me your sister in marriage.' But finally, on a night when they
were lying around in Kali's barnyard, sated with toddy, he
asked Muthu.

'Do you think I am a good man?'

'Why do you doubt that? You are a better man than me.'

'Are you just humouring me? Or are you being truthful?'

'Truly! I am ready to go to any temple and swear that you
are a good, good, good man.'

'Then, will you marry your sister to me?'

Muthu did not hesitate even for a minute. He said, 'Dey,
mapillai! Oh no, I cannot address my mapillai as "dey"! I
should say "Mr Mapillai"!' He went on and on, teasing Kali.

Kali assumed that it was the toddy that did the talking
and that Muthu would forget everything in the morning.
But the very next day, he spoke to his parents and sister,
and came back to Kali the same evening with their consent.
From then on, they started addressing each other as mapillai
and machan.

That night had been quite like this one. A waxing moon,
three-quarters its size, was throwing its light across the sky.
Muthu could hear Kali opening the makeshift gate to the

barnyard. He sat up. Kali came with a full bottle. 'This is Muniyannan's arrack. It is our luck this was available today,' he said and started pouring it.

They drank the arrack out of small earthen pitchers and cracked open peanut shells and popped the peanuts into their mouths. Muthu always drank it almost neat and also downed it all really fast. It sank down his throat with a sting. It was definitely good arrack. It would be good if Ponna came with the food before he went for the next round. He had a habit of holding his nose and swallowing it all in one go. Kali was different; he took his time with each glass and drank up to four or five. He preferred to feel the intoxication slowly growing inside him.

'Mapillai, the last two fasts have just not been the same without you. You must come this time. I will make sure no one bothers you. Tell me, will you come?'

Kali's eyes teared up and they shone in the moonlight. He was moved by Muthu's words.

'I will come, machan. I will,' he said.

'We can drink and make merry like we used to. Come. Tell me when you can come. I will get things ready . . .'

'When does your sister want to go?'

'It is you who has to decide that. She is scared of you. She has not come there for two years now. If you say yes, I will take her with me tomorrow.'

'All right. Take her with you. I will come on the day the gods go back uphill, stay for the last day and then return.'

Ponna brought dinner. Usually, when she came there, she

did not like anyone else hanging about. But today, it was her brother, Muthu, and he had come to speak for her. So she had cooked the dinner with care. Often, jobless fellows from the village would be sitting and chatting away with Kali. She would come there hoping to catch a private moment with Kali, and all her desire would vanish the moment she saw someone else. Those people weren't good at taking a hint and leaving the couple alone. She would wait impatiently, and finally leave without talking to him.

She would often explode, 'If someone comes, meet them at the gate, talk to them and send them away! These wretched people never leave once they come and sit inside the barnyard. They look at how good our cattle seem to be, and they go and talk about it to the entire village!'

She didn't mind Nallayyan. Even though the entire village talked ill of him, in her opinion he was good-hearted. He always had a kind word or two for Ponna. Once, when Uncle had come over, Ponna was on her way to the barnyard, carrying food, when she stopped to watch some children playing. What did children have to worry about? They could play all the time even in the streets. She too felt like playing along with them. But someone might remark, 'Now that she does not have a child of her own, she has decided to become one and prance about herself.' They might stop their children from talking to her. So Ponna contented herself with watching them from a distance. When she entered the barnyard, feeling content, she heard Nallayyan say, 'This is the kind of space you need for a calf to play around in.' A week-old calf was leaping about all over the barnyard.

'We have the space, Uncle, and we can rejoice at the calf's bounding about. After all, do we have children to run around this place?' she said in a tone of resignation.

Whenever this topic came up, Uncle had words that were like balm to her aching heart. In fact, she would often make some such remark just to elicit his response. And Uncle responded that day. He said, 'Don't worry, daughter-in-law. Enjoy the calf's happiness. That is a child, too. If you go out into the street, don't you see a number of children playing? Watch them as long as you want. That's enough. What else is there in a child? Everything lasts only a little while. Take this calf, for example. After some time, it will leap on to this cot. It will go and bother the goats. We will get annoyed and tie it up in one place. My brother's children used to come to my house. It would all be nice for a while. After that, it would all be a nuisance with them breaking this and smashing that. I would chase them away like dogs. They'd cry as they ran. So what? In their own homes, they behaved themselves. That's because if they broke anything, their mothers would take hot iron rods to them. So, it is better to look at it all from a distance. It is a nuisance to have to take care of children. Be relieved that you don't have to go through all that. Let stupid dogs who know nothing about happiness keep having children and keep suffering. Let us laugh at that too!'

'Are you always this playful, Uncle?' she asked.

'That is the key to happiness, dear girl. Take everything lightly, you will not be assailed by worries. Do not think about who says what. It balances out if we too talk ill of them!' he said.

Now, again, Ponna felt as happy in the barnyard as she was whenever Uncle Nallayyan visited. She hadn't been to the chariot festival for two years in a row. Her brother was not going to let that happen this time. She had cooked what her brother loved most: kootucharu and spicy vadai. As soon she set her basket down, Muthu said, 'Ponna, we will serve ourselves. You go back home. I have discussed everything with mapillai. He has said yes to your going with me in the morning.'

Though Muthu had told her this, she would only be convinced if she heard it straight from Kali. Would he really have agreed to send her on the day the gods went back to the hill? She felt like asking gleefully, 'Really?' But she wondered if that would be hurtful to Kali. He might say, 'Do you want it so badly?' Even if he did not say anything in her brother's presence, he would make sure he told her later. To break her silence, Muthu said, 'Mapillai, you tell her yourself. She will believe it only if you say it. My words don't carry weight any more.'

Kali laughed, 'Well, there are places where your words work wonders. Ponna, leave with your brother in the morning. I will come on the eighteenth day . . . We'll see.'

Not wanting to be in the way of their conversation, Ponna left right away. But a million thoughts assailed her. What did he mean when he said 'We'll see'? Was it in response to what her brother meant when he said 'I have discussed everything'?

Just a little while ago, when they were preparing dinner, her mother-in-law had told her, 'What is there to think about? This is god's work. You are going to be with whoever appears as god for you. God will show you the way. Do you know the old Vellapillai woman in our village? Do you know how her mother conceived her? She was given by god. Asking for a boy, her mother went there a second time too. And she got the male child she wanted. Ponna, this is a tradition that has been going on for ages. Don't worry about anything. Just think of god.'

As she walked back home, Ponna chanted to herself, 'Oh, Karattaiya, mother Devatha, it is in you that I trust. Please show me a good way.'

twenty

Once Ponna left, Kali refilled the pitchers and also took some food on his plate. He always liked to drink as he ate. But Muthu preferred to be done with all the drinking before getting to the food. Sometimes the food would stay untouched because he would have passed out after all the drinking. In some ways, he was much like the goat who was let out after being kept shut inside for a better part of the day. It would rush to the fodder and start munching it loudly. Muthu was exactly like that. Kali always laughed at his speed and urgency. As soon as he drank straight from the pitcher, Muthu opened his mouth wide to take a deep breath. The sting from the arrack reached his nose. He took a handful of pakodas and put them in his mouth.

Kali laughed. 'Eat slowly, machan. Do you think I won't leave anything for you?'

'You know me, don't you? This is nothing new to me,' said Muthu. Then he asked Kali, 'Mapillai, we gave our girl in marriage to you as soon as you asked, didn't we? Is it fair that you have not sent her home these past two years?'

'Is it fair that you didn't ask me this these past two years? Why are you so concerned suddenly?' Kali too spoke out.

'True. It was wrong on my part. I accept. I thought I should not interfere when there were elders to do that . . .' said Muthu.

Kali's voice rose in anger: 'What good are these elders for? They plan to pimp their own daughter and also come and tell me that shamelessly.'

Sensing a change in the air, the dog came running towards him, barked once, and moved away to lie down elsewhere. Having waited for just this kind of moment, Muthu spoke: 'Please don't say that, mapillai. It is because we couldn't bear to see you two suffer that we came up with that idea. This is nothing new, mapillai. It has been going on for ages now. We have gone there a few times too, haven't we?'

'You tell me. If your wife was childless, would you have sent her with a stranger?'

'Mapillai. Don't call him a stranger. Who remembers faces? All men are gods that night. Think of him as god, you might even feel happy about it. Isn't it a great blessing if our child comes from god? Haven't you heard people remark, "This child is a boon from god"? Those children were born exactly this way, mapillai.'

'When you and I went, were we gods? All we wanted was to find some decent-looking women to fuck, didn't we? Did you ever think of yourself as a god?'

'It does not matter what we thought of ourselves. If the women get children because of us, we become gods for them.'

'Really?! All men there are radiant with divinity, roaming around holding their cocks in their hands. It happened because people were ignorant in those days. Who will send their women now? Will you send your wife?'

'How much have you suffered these past twelve years because of this one issue?' reasoned Muthu. 'You lie confined to this barnyard and the field. This should end. We should be able to hold our heads high in front of others. If I were in such a situation, and if this were the only solution, then yes, I would send my wife.'

'You might,' countered Kali, 'I won't. Actually, if you were really faced with such a situation, I know you wouldn't either. You are now arguing for the sake of it. In those days, when a boy was a mere child, they got him married to a girl. In reality, it was the boy's father who did with the girl all that the husband was supposed to do. The boy was a husband just in name. Will such a thing be approved of today? This is just like that.'

'It is not like that. There are women who go to other men for various reasons. This is not like that. Here, as part of a festival, god gives a woman a blessing. I want you to become the Kali you used to be. And I want to see my sister happy again. That's why—'

'You are so old-fashioned, Muthu,' snapped Kali. 'Earlier, a woman could be with however many men as long as they were all from the same caste. Even related castes were fine. But if she went with an "untouchable", they excommunicated her. Is that how it works today? We insist that a woman should be with just one man from the same caste. Then how would this work? More than half the young men roaming about town are from the "untouchable" castes. If any one of them gets to be with Ponna, I simply cannot touch her after that. I cannot even lift and hold the child. Why do I need all that? I am happy lying around here. I don't want a child so desperately. Moreover, all of you will call me impotent and laugh at me. So, let it go.'

'When a woman goes secretly, who knows which caste the man belongs to? Also, it is a mistake only if others come to know of it. Anyway, if you don't want to do this, we won't. But please don't use this as a reason not to come home for the festival.'

'I will come. But let me be clear: I am not sending my wife anywhere.'

It was clear to Muthu that he could not shake Kali's conviction on this matter. But that didn't mean he would abandon the matter altogether. He knew he had to find another way to convince Kali. Before they went to bed after midnight, they spoke about other things. In the morning, Muthu woke up to the sound of the blackbird.

He roused Kali and said to him, 'Don't brood over anything. Come on the day the gods return to the hill. I will make excellent arrangements. Let's have fun!'

Kali saw him off at the gate. On his way out, Muthu was assailed by doubts as to whether he was right or wrong in what he was about to do. His justification to himself was that since he was doing it for a good reason, it must be the right thing.

'Mapillai said yes to everything, Ponna. I explained to him that this was a religious matter, and I made him agree. He loves you so much.' Saying this to Ponna, he took her with him at the crack of dawn.

Muthu knew that Kali and Ponna had not had a chance to speak to each other in private either the night before or in the morning. Now he had to make sure it did not happen until the task was done. Also, it was important that Ponna always thought of it as god's work. Kali could be handled. In fact, once a child was born, it might not even matter if he found out. None of these things might matter to him when a child called him 'Appa' and crawled on to his lap.

twenty-one

Kali was half-asleep on the cot under the portia tree when Muthu's voice woke him up.

'Welcome, mapillai. Have I made you wait for too long? These fellows never leave me alone. I had planned to stay put at home on this festival day, but who lets you be? You know Selvarasu, don't you? He wanted me to go with him to select a bullock. It took us so long to finish that transaction. The bullock looked like it was quite used to pulling carts. But it had only two teeth. The fellow wouldn't come down below forty rupees. We somehow agreed on thirty-five. All right, come. Let's eat. You could have eaten. Why should you be waiting for me?'

It was only when the two were alone that Muthu addressed Kali in the friendly terms reminiscent of their childhood days. But when Kali was here, he was the son-in-law, and Muthu's address shifted accordingly.

Kali rose from the cot, saying, 'Oh, I didn't mind waiting. And I dozed off.'

Portia leaves had been stitched together into a wide leaf

plate for them to eat from. At festival time, mendicants delivered stitched leaf plates to every home. But since they had a huge portia tree right in the front, the mendicants sat there in its shade and stitched their own leaves for them to use. So, they never ran out of these leaf plates.

Kali declined the snacks since he'd already eaten a lot of them. Muthu murmured in his ear, 'Don't eat too much. I have made other plans.' In times like these, Muthu's plans always excelled. He also didn't hesitate to spend. 'It is enough to leave a little for the children,' he always said. 'Don't we have to live well? The children can fend for themselves.'

After lunch, they sat under the portia tree and chewed betel leaves. Since they'd been bought just the day before at the Tuesday market, the leaves were fresh. Kali's mother-in-law was in the habit of chewing betel leaves every day. So, they always had enough at home. She wrapped the leaves in a white cloth and kept them on top of the water pot. She also wet the cloth two or three times a day so that the leaves wouldn't wilt until the next week's market.

'Mapillai, now we can go out for a while, can't we? I hope you have nothing planned,' said Muthu. 'Hang on a minute. We will leave soon,' he added and rushed inside. Kali heard him tell his mother, 'What, Mother? No, nothing at all.'

And then Kali heard his mother-in-law chastising Muthu, 'Why couldn't you come back sooner? These two are all over each other as if they just got married, and I got tired having to call Ponna to help me here. Nothing got done here. Anyway. I will take care. You fellows go.'

Muthu also said goodbye to Ponna who was arranging the pots and pans.

He rushed back to Kali and said, 'Come!'

Bored and lonely from sitting under the portia tree for so long, Kali was now ready to go out. In his barnyard, there was always some work to do. He felt that the most difficult thing to do was to do nothing at all. He knew Muthu had a knack for finding secret hideouts in the forest, and that he would also have furnished them with all that was needed whenever he spent time there.

There was a rocky patch in the elevated section of the fields. It was quite rugged and in the gaps between the huge rocks, giant trees stuck out forming bridges across the two rock faces. Only very rarely did someone go in there to defecate. And they were always afraid. But Muthu had a hideout even there, deep inside. There was a palm tree atop a pile of rocks, and he had worked using the rocks right below that palm tree. He had nudged them away with a crowbar and cleared a circular spot where five people could easily sit and two could lie down. But his genius lay in the way he had laid palm fronds on the trees that lay over the gap right above them, forming a bridge between the two rocks. Not only did this give them the much-needed shade but also served as a perfect decoy: for anyone who looked from above, it simply seemed as though the palm fronds had just fallen in the wind.

And all that Muthu needed was hidden in the crevices in the rocks: chilli, salt, a lead wok with a broken crimp, a mud pot—everything needed to run a small family. A rat, a bandicoot, a quail or a partridge would get fried in there now and then. Secret places were Muthu's happy places.

When Muthu took him in there once, Kali said, 'Dey, machan, why do you have this space? Which woman do you bring here?'

'Nothing like that, mapillai. People can spot if anyone comes and goes. Only I come here. You know my father, don't you? This is where I come to escape him,' Muthu replied.

Once, when they were preparing the land for sowing peanuts, Muthu bought a large pitcher of toddy and hid it in one spot. Two ploughs were working on the land. Once in a little while, Muthu ran to the rocky patch and while returning to the field, he made a show of tightening his loincloth and said, 'My stomach's upset.' But how many times could they halt the ploughing? Annoyed, his father ran after Muthu the next time he took off, and discovered his secret spot.

'Are you a rat?' he laughed. 'You have made a hideout in this little nook.'

After that, everyone started visiting the spot, if only to marvel at Muthu's genius. So he had to abandon that spot, but it was not as if there was a dearth of possible secret locations there.

There was certainly one spot that he'd had since childhood, which no one had been able to discover. Only Kali was privy to it. The elevated fields ended at the stream, the edge of which was bordered by ten large, fully grown neem trees. On one of those trees, Muthu had fastened two of the branches together to form a loft and had completed it using long stalks, ropes and plaited palm fronds. To an outsider, it would just look as though the neem branches had entwined. He could spend days and nights over there. He had also furnished the place with all the things he needed. Though he could not really cook there, he could pretty much do everything else he wanted to. If there was an argument or a fight at home, he would run away and spend at least a night and a day there. On one such occasion, they had looked for him everywhere, without any luck. After a whole night and a day, he returned home as if nothing had happened. But they still hadn't been able to locate this spot.

When Kali said, 'You should have been born a crow or a cuckoo,' he replied, 'I would have been much happier that way, you know.'

Muthu too had a barn, but it was his father who was the master there. He always remarked when he visited Kali's barn, 'Only children without their fathers around are the lucky ones.'

Remembering all this, Kali thought that they were now going to one such haven. But Muthu seemed to walk past all the fields. The sun had started going down, but in its slant it could be felt more sharply.

'How much further?'

'If you want to see a new place and taste new stuff, you should not mind such discomfort. Wait and see. You will hug me and give me a kiss!' said Muthu.

Kali's curiosity was piqued. He kept walking with Muthu past the barren lands.

twenty-two

Ponna's parents got busy as soon as Kali and Muthu left. 'We
are late,' they said to Ponna and rushed her to get ready.
Before he left, Muthu came into the house and said to
Ponna, 'We two will be fine. You go, Ponna. Think of god
in your mind.' She had stepped out eagerly to say bye to
Kali. He raised his eyebrows and smiled at her seductively.
He wouldn't talk to her when they were in a crowd or
even when there was anyone else around. But he would
communicate everything to her with his facial expressions.
His eyebrows would arch and talk to her; the curve of his lips
would contain his message for her; and just a nod of his head
would let her know what he wanted. It was only she who
was afraid that someone would catch them at this game. She
was surprised that her brother had managed to speak to Kali
and get his permission for this. After walking a little distance,
Kali turned to look at her. She stood right there, since she
knew he would do that. She sent him off with a shy smile.

A little while after their departure, a bullock cart pulled
up in front of the house. There was hay spread on the cart

for her and her mother to sit on. In the sack tied under the cart, there was some fodder for the bull and two coarse mats. Her mother had packed some food, and it was now next to her on the hay.

Ponna hadn't known her mother had packed food for the way, though she had been with her all day long. She must have soaked tamarind and made the rice when Ponna was busy with Kali.

'When did you manage to pack the food, Amma?' said Ponna.

'You two are all over each other like you just got married. You talk through signs. In the middle of all this, where do you have the time to pay attention to what I am up to?' her mother replied. 'If there is a child, it will teach you some modesty,' she added. 'Well, at least now your husband had the good sense to say yes. Pray that this time it should all go well.'

Ponna heaved a sigh of relief. When she had menstruated in the first month after the wedding, her mother-in-law sniggered in displeasure and turned her face away. Since then, the snigger had continued every month until that day. Nothing had happened to change that. But now, Ponna was going with her blessings. It was Kali's change of mind that was surprising to her. Perhaps it was because her brother and Kali were friends since childhood. That's why his words had had some effect.

In a very short while, the bullock cart reached the main road that was lined on both sides with huge tamarind trees. From the point where their mud path met this main road, they saw that it was already lined with bullock carts. Traffic was quite bad even on days when people went to see the chariot, but nothing compared to this day. Their cart too inserted itself into the line. They saw there were a lot of carts without roofs and which had only hay spread on them. There were only one or two bullock carts that had a covered box to sit in. In all of these, men, women and children were packed tight. Both mother and daughter felt strange that it was only their cart that was not crowded.

Every cart carried stacks of grass and fodder for the bulls. They could even hear the crowing of hens and roosters from under some of the carts. People would go see the gods that night and the next day they would offer pongal and sacrifice a rooster for the snake god in the forest. After they'd cooked and eaten, they'd wash and clean their utensils right there before leaving. Hundreds of roosters would be sacrificed the next day. Needless to say, it would be another crowded day in town.

Not only did the dust from the roads settle on their bodies, it also flew on to their faces and made it hard to breathe. People walking by the side of the carts did not mind this even one bit. They carried on as if the dust was nothing but holy ash smearing itself on them. Taking a cue from her mother, Ponna covered her face with her sari. It looked like her mother was wearing a faded sari. Maybe this was the best one she had. However tirelessly she worked in the fields, she was unable to wear good clothes. Nor was she keen on doing that.

Ponna remembered a story from last year. Apparently, when people went with their carts to load up on hay, a man came there to conduct an auction just for them. They did not want to get into an auction, so they all bought a sari each. Ponna was now wearing the sari that Kali had bought her from that sale. He always preferred light-coloured saris. She loved this one—a light sandalwood colour—and she was now concerned about it getting caked with dust. Thankfully, after a little distance, women were sprinkling water from either side of the road, helping the dust settle. This was a service that people from the villages along the road took on during the festival season.

There were also water pandals every few miles or so. They were made by plaiting palm fronds together and then fastening them with coconut fronds. Two or three carts pulled up in front of each of the pandals. Everyone could get as many pitchers of cold water as they needed. Some people removed themselves to the other side of the pandals and drank water out of palm-fruit shells. Some of the pandals even had watery buttermilk in pots. This was like nectar to someone in thirst. Nothing could compete with that. Watching everyone around her, Ponna was filled with the excitement of a child.

The young men who drove the carts were keen on overtaking the carts ahead of them. Every time they managed to do that, all the young men and the children in that cart would shout and jeer at the one they overtook. All of this took a toll on the poor bullock that heaved, panted and struggled. Excitement pulsed through the entire stretch of the road. Ponna's father drove slowly and carefully. It was enough if they reached when there was still some daylight left. After all, there was nothing new about the festival that he needed to see after all these years. The last time he went was when he took little Ponna to see the festival. The years had rolled by. Now, looking at this crowd, Ponna had little doubt that all sorts of rules would be broken that night. Perhaps different rules applied to crowds?

Just like this road, the other roads that led to Karattur from all the other villages around it would also bring in similar crowds. Would the four quadrangle streets be enough to accommodate the thousands of people pouring into town? Just for this day, the town would expand into the distant lands surrounding it. The noise of the crowds continued to ring in her ears.

Her father stopped the cart at a water pandal. They could get watery buttermilk there! They only said it was watery, but it turned out to be excellent buttermilk. If you drank a small pitcher full of this, it would relieve not only your thirst but your hunger too. Nearby, there was also a large tank filled with water for the cattle. While the passengers were busy drinking the buttermilk, some of the drivers unharnessed their bullocks and took them for a drink of water.

All of these were acts of service that people from the villages along the road took upon themselves. These pandals lasted the entire duration of the festival. On some days, you could get not only water and buttermilk, but also panagam, sweetened with jaggery. All the palm-tree climbers of that village made sure that enough Karuppatti jaggery was available to make panagam in large vessels. When they were heading back to the cart, a man approached them. He was wearing a dhoti around his waist and had a folded towel under his arm. When he said, 'Samee . . .' Ponna's father turned around. 'What?' He could tell who the man was.

He said, 'Samee, the little ones are unable to walk. If you can give us a little space in your cart, you will be blessed.'

'Where will you sit?' Ponna's father asked.

'Samee, you go to the back and sit restfully on the hay. I will drive the cart and have these three sit next to me.'

'Are you a good driver?'

'Samee, I work for Periyasami's farm in Veliyur. My name is Maran. You can ask him. Everyone speaks highly of my work, samee. I will be gentle on the bulls. You will have nothing to fear.'

'All right. Come. Get in carefully,' said Ponna's father, handing over the reins to Maran. Moving the bull on the right slightly aside, Maran climbed on to the driver's spot. Then he lifted his two little children and made them sit. His wife was a little on the heavier side. She hoisted herself up by placing one foot on the pivot of the wheel and sat herself behind her husband, making sure she did not touch anyone sitting on the hay spread. Since now an entire family was to the front of the cart, the weight imbalance bothered the bullocks. So, Ponna's father moved further to the back to make it easier for them. Now they also had people to talk to.

twenty-three

It made Ponna anxious when her father started asking Maran about his family. Her fear was that once that ended, Maran might reciprocate. Gradually, it would come to his asking, 'How many children does your daughter have?' And when they would hear she had no children yet, they would take pity on her and suggest some medicine or some ritual. 'I have nothing but humiliation to expect, even from a farmhand,' she thought. She did her part to make sure the conversation did not head that way. Thankfully, her father started talking about cultivation instead.

The two children were very beautiful. The one sitting on the father's lap must have been eight years old. A small kandangi cloth torn from a sari was all she was wearing around her waist. The other one, sitting naked on her mother's lap, must have only been three. Ponna felt like keeping the baby on her lap. But caste laws forbade her from touching the child. She refrained from even playing with caste children, since she feared some rebuke or comment.

In the month of Purattasi, it was a tradition to offer pongal at the Perumal temple at the foot of a hill. At the crack of dawn, if one took the shortcut, one could reach the temple by the time the sun was overhead. Of course, if someone was going like this by bullock cart, you could all go together. Earlier, Kali used to take the initiative to arrange for and even drive the cart. Those were very happy journeys. He would take as many people as the cart could hold. If they left very early, they would be at the foot of the hill by the time it was bright and sunny. The hill was basically a bare rock that resembled a giant basket that had been turned upside down. The region surrounding the hill was all forest. On the Saturdays of the Purattasi month, crowds from nearby flocked to the temple. You could see stoves busy preparing pongal for the offering. The sambar made with green gram dal, pumpkin and ladies' fingers—all specially made for this offering for Vishnu—were delicious. Everyone followed the same recipe.

On the mud roads leading to that hill, one could never spot any sign of a human dwelling. It was all green and lush vegetation. Elevated fields cultivating groundnuts dotted the edges of the roads and filled everyone with joy. And the plants that yielded thurvarai dal stood with their leaves spread out like the unfurled tails of proud peacocks. It was soothing to the heart just to drive on this road. Ponna had promised three head shaves and three pongal offerings to this deity. When would she get to complete that?

Once during their trip there, Kali's cart was so crowded that they were practically elbowing each other for space.

Accompanying them from Vandukkaadu were Kannaaya and her two children. Her son, who was three or four years old, was dark and snot constantly dribbled from his nose. The girl was an infant; she hadn't even started to crawl. Kannaaya was struggling to take care of the children while also holding on to all the things she was carrying for the temple offering. Her husband was walking behind the vehicle, since there was absolutely no space for him in it. Ponna took the infant from Kannaaya and kept it on her lap, making sure the sun didn't bother the baby. The child was in utter delight at the vehicle's bouncing up and down on the road, and it laughed whenever Ponna made a 'kooooo' sound twirling her tongue around.

Kannaaya's wedding had happened only a year after Ponna's, but she already had two children one after the other. Whenever Ponna saw someone like that, she shrank from within. Despite her best efforts to cheer up, she would be sad the whole day. There were no words to describe the pride and joy glowing on the faces of women who managed to have a child within a year of their marriage. They also overdid it in front of Ponna. The baby, who was laughing until then, suddenly grunted. Ponna saw that the baby had defecated, wetting the little white cloth tied around her waist.

The stench was overpowering. What had Kannaaya eaten before feeding the child? Ponna's sari too was wet with the child's faeces. 'Why does it stink so badly? Did you eat anything that you were not supposed to during the festival weeks?' Ponna asked as she handed over the baby to Kannaaya. She could not bear the stench and the dampness on her sari. Everyone in the cart felt assailed by it and were trying to manage it by covering and twitching their noses. Kali stopped the cart at a well by the side of the road. Ponna ran to the well, took some water from the large water holder next to it and cleaned herself. Kannaaya cleaned the child's legs and feet and also rinsed the cloth it was wearing.

Why carry the baby when she was travelling so far? Was the god going to be mad if she decided to come the next year instead? All right, if she still chose to go, shouldn't she know what to feed the child before travel? Ponna was really annoyed. It felt like the stench from her sari had not fully gone.

'This is making me retch. Kannaaya, don't you think you should feed the infant something she can digest?' she said.

And Kannaaya retorted, 'Shit will stink. Is it only my baby's shit that stinks? Does yours smell wonderful? You'd know if you'd had and raised a child of your own. You keep saying it stinks, as if I don't know it!'

The worst thing was not Kannaaya's remark that Ponna didn't know what it took to raise a child. It was what Kannaaya muttered under her breath after that, which everyone heard anyway: 'This childless woman smells a child's ass and squirms at the sight of a child's shit. How does she expect to be blessed with a child?'

Ponna broke into sobs. Kali did not know what to do. He just made a general remark: 'Can't you keep quiet? These women! They can never keep their tongues under control.' But the argument had rippled out among the other passengers by then, and they took sides.

'Once you have a child, you will have things like shit to deal with. You can't be squeamish about that.'

'Well, you promptly lifted the child and gave it to its mother. Whom can she hand it over to in turn? Nobody. She has to do it herself, doesn't she?'

It turned out that Ponna was more upset with the words of those who claimed to speak in support of her than those who took Kannaaya's side.

'Who knows what curse it is that has kept her childless and suffering? How can you speak to her like that?'

'Had she handled a child before, she would have done better. She didn't know. That doesn't mean you call her barren.'

'Don't cry, Ponna. This time next year Perumalsami would have given you a child.'

Until they reached the temple, this was their only topic of conversation. Ponna was mad at Kali. Not only had he given Kannaaya a ride in the cart, he had also included Ponna in his admonition.

'Do I have a problem controlling my tongue? What about what the other woman said?' Ponna said. She had long since lost interest in the deity, in climbing the hill and in making pongal. But she did it anyway just for the sake of it. Thankfully, when they got ready to leave, Kannaaya did not join them. Her husband informed them that they were going to stay on longer. They might have chosen a different cart to return by. On the way back, everyone in Ponna's cart scolded the absent Kannaaya: she talked back, she was arrogant, she was haughty—all sorts of words rolled around.

But Ponna knew that they felt obliged to speak against Kannaaya because they were in Ponna's vehicle. When they would meet Kannaaya, they would talk ill of Ponna.

She did not speak to Kali for a month after this event. 'If I had simply taken your side in front of everyone,' he said, 'wouldn't they have said I was merely taking my wife's side? That's why I made a general remark. She is an uncouth woman. Why are you taking her words so seriously?' But still she did not speak to him. She felt isolated from everyone and confined herself to the house. She also took to sleeping at odd hours. Sometimes she cooked, at other times she forgot to. She didn't go anywhere near the field or the barnyard. Her face looked swollen most of the time, her hair dishevelled. Normally, she wouldn't even allow him to leave his hair untied. She would also wash his hair for him. But now she did nothing. When he came home, she laid food on his plate. When she forgot to make any food at all, Kali's mother brought his food. Now he mostly ate his mother's food. It also became very difficult to make her eat.

Kali and his mother were quite alarmed seeing her lie around with no sense of day or night. They feared she might be possessed by some evil spirit. They even thought of sending for her parents. When Kali came home at midnight and knocked on the door, it took her a long time to unlock it. She looked demented. Her arms, which once used to embrace him with desire, now lay limp and dead. Kali was frustrated. But just when he was at a loss to figure out what to do, something happened that revived her.

A goat in the barn was in the throes of a difficult birthing. Kali ran to Ponna, imploring her, 'You used to take such loving care of it, calling it your goat, remember? You used to say, "It doesn't matter that I don't have children. My goats and cows will always yield abundantly." Now will you consider going to the barn and taking care of the goat in its suffering and give it some strength? Or are you going to let it die? It is a struggle of two lives now. Kattu Karuppanarayya! Show us a good way. Badrakali! Be on my side, Mother!'

The moment she heard that, she rose as if she had just regained consciousness and ran to the barn. Even after the kid had been force-delivered, the goat's legs were shaking. For the next ten days, until it was able to get up on its own feet and look at its young one, Ponna stayed in the barnyard. She washed the goat with warm water twice a day. She ground the pulp of aloe vera and applied it on the goat's wounds from the delivery. She fed it steamed kambu millets. It was her love for this mother-goat that revived her. The next year, when he brought up the subject of going to the Perumal temple, she retorted, 'Why? So that you can bring some woman along to humiliate me?' and, instead, walked all the way to the temple. She also stopped lifting and holding anyone's children. Their barnyard always had little calves and kids for her to play with.

twenty-four

Ponna loved the eyes of the little child who, sitting on her mother's lap, kept looking at Ponna. The child smiled through her eyes. In her mind, Ponna lifted the child and kissed her. Maran drove the cart faster than her father did. He was also able to overtake some of the other vehicles with great ease. For all this, he didn't land the whip on the bullocks even once. All he did was touch them on their flanks with the handle of the whip. He seemed to be adept at the language of the animals, and since he was busy with the driving, his conversation with her father did not continue. It was a relief to her.

As they neared the town, she could see the hill at a distance through the gaps in the tamarind trees en route. Atop the hill, like a hand folded in prayer, was the barren rock. The hill's peak was resplendent in the receding light of the day.

Ponna prayed: 'If you do not show me a way this time, the only option I have is to fall from that hilltop . . . I am coming today to see the god. I might fail to recognize you. You have to help me. You have to give me a child. I do not know in what form you will come today, where you will stand, what you will say, and how you will approach me. Kali's hands are like large, rugged sieves. When they touch my cheek, my love pours forth despite the roughness of their touch. How will your touch be? How will you enter my body? I know nothing, but I am coming now, trusting you . . . My husband's permission to this is not whole-hearted. He has said yes because my brother asked for it. Just like you, he wants to keep me in his body. He would never want to tear me apart from his body and give me to someone else. Despite all that, I am coming to you now. Let him hold his head high among people. Let him not stay confined to the barnyard, let the spring be back in his gait. May his embrace regain the love it used to have. You have to help us be like others, be accepted by everyone, my Father . . . my Mother . . .'

Her mind was immersed in prayers.

She felt as though a new power was entering her. She felt dizzy, so she lay on her mother's lap. Though she could not shrink herself and lie like a baby, it was comforting to lie with her head in her mother's lap. She even forgot that this was the same mother who had been annoying her the whole morning. After a long time, she felt her mother's gentle hands on her back. Her mother's hand had sacred threads wrapped around the wrist, and she relished this maternal touch. Her mother's eyes had teared up thinking about something. It seemed that a mother needed the joy of having a child, and the child that of having a mother.

Nallayyan used to say, 'Why do you think we have and raise children? For them to grow up well? No. We do it because we seem to need it for ourselves. That is why we have children and raise them. And then in old age we complain that those children are not taking care of us. This is all plain madness . . .'

Let him be right. We don't expect our children to take care of us when we are old. It is enough if we can have a social life because of them. Now we are forced to act like untouchables, fearing if our sight or touch is inauspicious. All we want is to show these people who ostracize us that we too are people just like them.

Her mind was filled with various confusing dreams. There was one in which she walked a long distance with a child across her shoulder. It occurred to her that she could never see the child's face. Was it even her child? From the way she walked, it looked like she had stolen the baby from somewhere. Was that true? Why was Kali never part of this particular vision? Where had he gone? Did he abandon her thinking that she didn't need him when she had a child? With images and memories mingling with one another, she lay on her mother's lap, tossed between sleep and wakefulness.

There was a lot of noise. Above the din of carts pulling over, the voices of people could be heard. They sounded unintelligible, like the cawing of crows at dawn. Maran drove the cart into the market, which seemed to be in full swing already. Ponna's mother woke her up only after Maran pulled over at a spot wide enough for their cart. It took her a while to get her bearings. She couldn't remember how long she had slept in her mother's lap. She was fully awake only after a little while. The sun was down, and the shadow of twilight spread over everything. She covered her bosom properly, wiped her face with the end of her sari and, holding her mother's hand, got off the cart. She saw that the market was filled with people and cattle. She was amazed. Had the heavens landed here? She hadn't seen this much of a crowd even on the days when people came to see the chariot. If there were already so many people here, how many more must be coming through the roads leading up to here from all four directions! Ponna looked at everything with a great sense of wonder.

'Samee,' Maran said with great reverence, 'may you be blessed. But for your help, we couldn't have made it all the way with these children. It is Devatha herself who showed you to us at the right time. She has somehow brought us here. Please let me know if you need any work done. When there is no work at my landlord's farm, I will work for you. It is people like you that I should serve.'

His wife bent low in obeisance and said, 'We will take leave.' Ponna's mother undid a knot at the end of her sari, took out an anna and gave it to Maran's wife, who received it in her pallu. They walked backwards for a few steps before walking away.

While Maran and his wife were taking their leave, their little child had been smiling at Ponna. It was a good omen. Ponna had wanted to affectionately pinch the child's cheek.

Until the family vanished into the crowds, she kept looking at the child. Please bless me with such a charming child, my lord, she prayed.

Her father untied the bullocks from their harness. Bringing them around, tied to the front of the harness, he threw some fodder for them to gorge on. As darkness settled in, fire torches started glowing here and there in the market. Human faces became wandering figures of smoke. Her mother opened the food package. To Ponna, everything appeared foggy. She perceived everything as images from a dream that was not even hers.

twenty-five

Muthu and Kali walked along the meandering paths and elevated boundaries between the fields. They were enveloped in a variety of sounds—birds settling on the palm trees, the rustle of dry leaves in the mild wind, the sound of palm fronds grating against each other. Intertwined with all of these, their voices too had lost their human quality. Though Kali had been to these places several times when they were children, he was now unable to guess where Muthu was taking him. So much had changed in all the years he had stayed shut inside his barn.

They walked past fields belonging to both villages and reached the stream. It was flanked by thick bushes on both sides. The avaram shrubs had grown as tall as trees. Muthu walked past them, suddenly turned a corner and climbed higher. There was a coconut grove in front of Kali's eyes. There must have been a hundred trees. They had been planted following the dictum that there must be enough space between two coconut trees for a chariot to pass through. Almost all the trees were of the same height. He could even see the tender coconut and the toddy pots on many of them. He had never seen such a grove in these parts. When all the elevated fields lay dried up, how did such a coconut grove thrive here?

For most other crops, you could manage even if you had very little water in the well. It could even be as little as what a small cuckoo would need for a drink. With that you could grow some chilli, a square-measure of raagi or some cotton. But coconut trees needed plenty of water. Otherwise, the coir covering would dry and hang, and that in turn would make the top of the tree shrivel up. Such trees looked like broken-winged birds frozen in mid-air. Kali had four coconut trees. In the rainy season, he would widen the circle around the tree for it to hold more water. But in summer, the circle would shrink close to the roots, and he would release two loads of water through the little canal. How much of it would get to the coconut trees? Not much. Kali called this 'Life Water'. This water was meant to give just enough strength to the coconut trees to survive. He'd do that because they needed coconut for their food. Ponna would also sell what she didn't need. After all, it was only the two of them.

But Kali could not get over his sense of wonder that here, in this dry land, was a coconut grove with a hundred trees. As they entered, a chill palm breeze took them in its embrace. Dried-up barks and fallen fronds had been stacked up on a side. Some fronds had also been spread under each tree. He was full of questions: 'Machan, who owns this place? I never realized there was such a grove so close to us. There would be a hundred trees, right? Looks like they have all ripened. What do they do for water?'

Muthu told him the story of that place. A Muslim merchant who owned a cotton storehouse in Karattur also owned this place. Before this grove of trees came up, this too was a dry piece of land like the surrounding stretches. But the cotton merchant had a lot of money. He brought a farming family from yonder and gave them a place to live here. This family had been languishing in a farm there, working as farmhands. He had met them during his visits there to buy cotton. When he called them here to take care of the place, they moved. Since he had no major concerns regarding money, he gave them what they needed. There were three wells for this land, and one well was used for irrigation every day. What more did the trees need? There was also a tile-roofed house right in the middle of the property for the owner to stay in when he visited occasionally. The family stayed in the thatched-roof hut. The moment the flower sheath started showing and the trees started yielding, a family of traditional tree climbers also found its way into the grove. Not only did they take over the trees but they also started making and selling toddy.

Kali's mouth watered at the thought of the toddy. Until some years ago, you could get coconut toddy in shops. You could drink a bellyful at whatever time you wanted to; it was not as sharp as palm toddy. It was, in fact, sweet. But it was a real shock when all toddy and arrack businesses in Sailam district were ordered to be shut down. One could not see toddy bowls on trees. The family was at a loss about what to do; it had been their traditional livelihood. Life, in general, lost its flavour. So, people started brewing arrack in secret. But there was a persistent fear of the police. People wondered why some local educated groups were making these decisions. In the middle of the white man's rule, who suddenly gave these people the power? How else would things turn out if this lawyer from Sailam—a man who knew nothing about alcohol, who had never tasted meat in his life—was made the minister?

Also, this order was only for Salem district. No other place had such a rule. It was supposed to be a favour this lawyer had done for his district. Could everybody afford to go to the district of Konamputtur next door just to drink? But some people did. Thankfully, the lawyer went away soon and the white man's rule was back again. Although the shops didn't open again, the rules were relaxed. Nonetheless, Kali hadn't drunk toddy in a long while.

Delighted that Muthu had brought him to the right place, he put his arm around Muthu's shoulders and they walked towards the end of the grove, next to the stream, where the family of tree climbers lived. This was a small, thatched-roof hut. Little mud toddy pots had been kept upside down in front of it. There were also four or five mats for people to sit on.

By the time they reached there, the day was casting a yellow light everywhere. Inside the grove, the light came filtered in thin rays. Two children were happily playing around. When Kali and Muthu sat down on the mats in front of the hut, they could hear sounds from inside, of dishes banging against each other.

'Who's there?' Muthu asked.

'Please sit, brother. I'll be there in a minute,' a voice replied from inside.

She stepped out saying, 'What happened, brother? You have come so late.' And Kali recognized her immediately.

'Katthayi! What are you doing here?' he said in amazement.

'Do you know her already?' Muthu said to him.

Kali just said, 'Hmm,' and turned to look at her. 'Where is Mandayan?' he asked.

'He went saying he wanted to have a word with the farm owner. Let me call him,' she said and walked a little distance into the grove. Then she called out to her husband, 'Pilla! Pilla!'

That was how she called her husband. If he was nearby, she would use one of her children's names to address him. Since it sounded like he had responded, she returned to the hut.

'How long have you been here?' Kali asked her.

Katthayi poured out her woes: 'It is in this dark place that we have been languishing for two years now. We used to live with other people; now we are all alone by ourselves. After that wretched whore made sure we got out of your land, we roamed around all over the place before landing here.'

twenty-six

Four or five years ago, Mandayan and Katthayi had come to Kali's land to climb palm trees, and they had stayed there for some days. They were newlyweds then. Katthayi's beauty was undisturbed. Mandayan had left his village because of a feud with his brothers. Deciding that they would make their living elsewhere, they had come to Kali's village. After all, a toddy tapper could find work to do wherever there were palm trees. All he needed was a strong rope and a sharp knife. Just like the gypsies, they could set up a hut with a few dried fronds on any rock they found. It was not very difficult.

Mandayan was very good with palm. He had acquired a deep understanding of the palm tree from a very young age. There had been trees that people had given up on, which Mandayan revived and made them spring toddy again. He was also excellent with working with the coir sheaths. Palm toddy was just as sweet as coconut toddy. If you tasted the top layer of alkali, it tasted as sweet as cane juice. The jaggery that came out of this just melted in your mouth. Since he was a master of all this, there was no village where he could not make a living.

They made a hut on a piece of rock on Kali's land. Half the produce was toddy, and the rest was the clear alkaline water. Katthayi's job was to boil and reduce the latter into jaggery. Most of the toddy was for consumption within Kali's property. But whatever was left of it, Mandayan sold to daily-wage labourers.

A man by the name Pazhani was doing similar work in the adjacent plot of land. His wife was a troublemaker. She decided that her business was not going to flourish as long as Mandayan and Katthayi were around. After all, it was not as if a lot of men came to drink every day. And how hard it was sometimes to get the money from them! One had to practically untie their loincloths and take the money out. And who needed a competitor in the middle of all this?

The day fresh toddy was brought down was when they could sell and make some money. Though some people drank on credit, there was quite a crowd on Tuesdays, the day of the market. The list of creditors was quite long, but if the owners persisted in asking the customer each time, it was possible they cleared their tabs. There was a caste dimension to this too. While it was easy to handle most customers, it was quite a challenge extracting money out of the farmers. But they expected you to pour toddy whenever they came.

As far as palm jaggery was concerned, it had to be preserved well and sold when the prices were good. Sometimes it would take even a year to see any profit. Either way, it was toddy that sold easily. So there was always some competition.

Pazhani's wife started making insinuations and hurling indirect abuses. She spread rumours linking Katthayi with each of her customers.

'Do you think she just sells toddy like I do? No! She bewitches the men. That's why these fellows go to her grinning from ear to ear.'

'She takes her customers into the hut. Who knows what she shows them there?'

'If she goes aside and removes her sari, milk oozes from her breasts. Mine are dry and shrivelled. Who will come for these?'

How long could Katthayi bear these insults? Since she was a new, young bride, she was not armed with words to retaliate with. But Pazhani's wife had no problem unleashing vulgarisms. Katthayi felt that it was better to die than to have to survive putting up with all this. Her eyes reddened because of crying every day. Mandayan was not the confrontational type. Also, if someone came to fight with you, you could argue it out. But if they implied, insinuated and said things here and there, how could one respond to that? However, it didn't mean they could ignore her, thinking of her as the dog that barked at the sun.

Mosalan frequented Mandayan's shop and stayed till late at night drinking. Pazhani's wife, the demoness, went to Mosalan's wife and said, 'Katthayi is being kept by your husband. Otherwise, why is he there in the grove till midnight?' Mosalan's wife came with a broomstick to assault

Katthayi. Mandayan and Katthayi abandoned the trees just when they were ripe with new toddy, and left the village. Kali couldn't do anything. How could he respond to someone who did not engage in direct combat but attacked by slandering and bad-mouthing? Also, if Kali did intervene, the woman might say, 'Look at this! The impotent one has come to fight!'

In fact, Kali heard what she said about him: 'This impotent man has brought her from somewhere. When his own wife is a dry land, what is he going to do with this new one?' He felt such rage that he wanted to drag that coarse and uncouth woman by her hair and give her a thrashing. But Ponna was firm. She said, 'Let's not get into this fight between the tree climbers. They think one thing when they climb up, and another when they climb down. Be careful.'

After all that time, Mandayan was very excited to see Kali. He had two tiny little children. Kali could not take his eyes off them. He sighed. What was the use of being so well built and strong enough to knock four men down in one blow? Mandayan was fat and short. So what? He had fathered two children. Perhaps his body was as dexterous as his hands. The children looked as beautiful as sculptures.

'Is he related to you?' Mandayan asked Muthu, referring to Kali.

'Related? Hey, Mandaya! Ponna is my own sister!' Muthu laughed.

'Somehow, we never got to know that. Otherwise, we could have brought him here long ago and given him a taste of the coconut toddy.'

As per Muthu's arrangement, they had steamed mochai peas and rice. Mandayan had coconut toddy as well as arrack soaked in coconut toddy to offer. Kali said, 'I will have the toddy first.' He was already regretting the fact that he had missed tasting the fish that would be available near the temple hill, now that the festival was coming to a close. The moon had started to ascend the skies.

twenty-seven

The marketplace was full of flame torches. In the brightness of those flames, the light from the little lamps that hung under the carts appeared muted. Her mother decided to open the packed food, knowing that it would take a long time to walk around the streets and then return. Ponna was not hungry; all she felt was a tightening of her stomach, but she ate whatever her mother put on her plate. Whenever her mother packed food for just one or two days, she added onions. It had a distinctly wonderful taste. But right now Ponna could not taste anything.

Her father decided not to go into the market. 'I have seen it for so many years,' he said. 'Who wants to walk all the distance now? It tires my legs. You two go. I will guard the vehicle.'

He kept repeating to them that they should be very careful when they went into the crowd. He asked them to be mindful of the chain and the taali pendant round their necks. He then told his wife not to keep money tied to the end of her sari, but to keep it in a pouch and tuck it into her garment close to her waist. 'All sorts of thieves will be roaming around today.' Then he added in a muffled voice, 'Cover your chest properly. These dogs have wandering hands.'

He wouldn't sleep so easily. If he stood around with the others minding their cart and bullocks, he wouldn't know how time went by. Finally, he asked them to return to this spot if they lost each other in the crowd.

Her mother lost her patience. 'Come, let's go. He'll keep telling us something or the other as though we are little children.' She dragged Ponna along and stepped into the market.

It was an ocean of human faces. Little patches of darkness lay here and there, challenging the light from the flame torches. Human bodies were rubbing, banging and pushing against one another. To Ponna, they all looked like worms crawling on top of each other.

'Don't think this is the only crowded place!' her mother said to her. 'Today, the entire town is like this everywhere, on all four sides. Even children and old people from the nearby villages have come. Take a look.' But all that she said was mere meaningless noise to Ponna's ears.

They walked past the market and arrived at a corner that was lit by five lanterns hung on large iron rods. These were permanent lanterns. But to manage the extra crowd, more light was needed. So, there were flame torches or more lanterns kept at regular intervals. There were also men in charge of these lamps, and they were running around making sure every place was lit. Right below the bunch of five lanterns were three flower shops. Ponna's mother bought some jasmine and kanakambaram flowers strung together and decorated Ponna's head with it.

It was only rarely that Ponna wore flowers. When she went to some function, she wore just a pinch of a flower. In her opinion, her lacklustre hair—ravaged by the sun and the heat and all the wandering around in the fields—didn't deserve to be decorated with flowers. In the early days of their marriage, Kali really liked it when she wore flowers. He'd pluck wild jasmine from creepers growing over the bushes in the fields and bring them home. They were small but incredibly fragrant. If she wore even ten of those flowers on her head, people four houses away were drawn by the scent. The local belief was that that particular flower's scent attracted snakes. So she asked Kali not to go looking for the creepers.

Some days, he brought cactus flowers. Those too were found on the edges of the fields. The plant was prickly, and the flower was mild ochre in colour. It did not have much of a fragrance, but if she brought it close to her nose, it smelled of sour toddy. It was really beautiful to look at, and a handful of the flowers made a lovely string. To avoid having to go looking for flowers, Kali brought some kanakambaram plants and a jasmine creeper and planted them along the little canal. In just a few days, they burst forth with blossom. Then it became a major task for Ponna to pluck them, string them together and to comb her hair just to wear the flowers. She was enthused at first, but the novelty soon wore off. Those who wanted flowers came to pluck them from the plants. They blossomed abundantly. She'd stand under the shrub and lament, 'The plant that we plant grows; the seed that we sow blooms; is it only me who is the wasted land here?'

Shouldn't she have given Kali a child at least in thanks for his love for her?

A lot of people were bathing in the pond. Even in summer, the pond was more than half full with water. All it needed was one rain, and water from all over town would flow into the pond. The place was well lit on all four sides. The workers were chasing away those who were jumping into the pond, and asking the spectators to keep moving. There were many men and far fewer women bathing in the pond. Whenever she looked at the pond, Ponna was reminded of the incidents involving Kali's grandfather, which his grandmother had told them about.

twenty-eight

On one such day several years ago, Sadayappan, Kali's grandfather, went to see the festivities. Though quite short in stature, he was a very shrewd man. It was the day the big chariot was brought out.

The British officer who had come to ensure law and order arrived near the holy pond with his retinue of lower officers. He was an enthusiastic man and loved contests. Seeing the number of people gathered for the festival, he began to think of some kind of a contest or another. That year, the pond was so full that waves rolled on it. There had been two or three excellent bouts of summer rain. There was quite a crowd at the pond in the daytime. On one side, five or six boys were throwing stones into the water. The aim was to see who could throw the farthest. That gave the British officer an idea and he sent out an announcement with the parai drum the very next day.

The news reached several villages. The news was that on that day, when the gods would return to the hills, a stone-throwing contest would be held on the banks of the temple pond. All contestants had to stand on one side of the pond and aim their stones towards the opposite bank. The stones should reach the other side of the tank without falling into the water. All those who managed to do that would receive one rupee as prize. And all those who lost would receive a whiplash right away right there next to the temple pond. Everyone would get three chances. It seemed that the idea was to design a contest which nobody could win.

The contest was all everybody could talk about that year. One rupee was a big amount. Some people who were determined to win the prize landed up at the temple pond the day before the actual contest and started practising their throws. The British officer had to issue an order prohibiting it.

The next day, a great crowd gathered around the pond. They had all come to watch the contest. The contestants themselves were hesitant. For, if they lost, they'd have to endure a whiplash, though the officer had ordered that the whiplash should not be so severe that it peeled away the skin on their backs but should merely create a sound effect. Gradually, the contestants started stepping out of the crowd. They had to stand on the east bank and aim their stones on the west bank. The stones were big and round like ostrich eggs, the kind of stones one used for the game of fifth stone.

Many started receiving whiplashes. Only one or two stones managed to cross even half the length. This provided the entire day's entertainment for the people. The moment someone received a slightly severe whiplash, his friends and relatives were outraged: 'Wretched white dog! Isn't there a limit to the game? He wants to throw stones from this side to the other. May stones fall upon his house! May people throw stones at him!' But they continued to stand and watch the rest of the contest.

The British officer did not budge from his spot. Even when he dismounted the horse, he stood right there. Since he could not bear the heat, he constantly drank something or the other. When the heat got too much for him, men came running, stood by his sides and fanned him. It was an imported fan made of palm fronds and had beautiful pictures drawn on it. The contest had started in the morning, and even by the afternoon, no one had won. The officer could not stop grinning. When he realized no one was going to win, he increased the prize money to ten rupees. He wanted to make more people participate and watch them receive whiplashes.

The moment they heard of the new prize money, a new line of contestants got ready. These men, with their dhotis tied tight around their loins and their turban cloth tied around their waist in deference, and running to throw stones, must have looked like bizarre creatures from another world. Every time someone lost and was given a whiplash, the officer smiled. If someone's stone managed to cross more than half the distance across the pond, he raised his eyebrows in wonder.

Kali's grandfather, Sadayappan, arrived there only in the late afternoon. Seeing the crowd around the pond, he inquired what was going on and watched the contest for a little while. After walking around the pond twice, he decided to participate. He was used to taking aim and throwing stones. He had practised it while herding goats in the forest. He could aim a stone sharply at a goat's hind leg. Most of the time, his stones could cross a square measure, which was over half an acre. Whenever he aimed a stone into the lake, at least one dead fish rose to the surface. All those who had come with him from the village now whistled and cheered him on.

He removed his dhoti and towel and stood in his loincloth, which was strung on a thread made of aloe fibre. It was wide in the front, and at the back, it hung like a long tail. His appearance was a source of mirth for the officer. Sadayappan felt like telling him, 'I feel like laughing looking at you, officer, wearing so many clothes in this heat.' But if he even smiled, the officer would detect the sarcasm in it, and that would blow up into a big problem. So, he controlled himself.

He stood on the farther edge of the east bank of the pond and came running at great speed towards the water. He looked like a bandicoot rolling down. Everyone looked silently at the pond. His stone flew more than halfway across and fell into the water with a plop. No one else had managed to reach his stone that far in his very first throw. The crowd clapped and cheered. The officer couldn't laugh now. With his mouth open in wonder, he kept staring at Sadayappan, who now came running again from the outer edge of the bank to cast his stone. Everyone was keen to find out how far this one would go. It crossed three-fourths of the distance before falling into the water with a splash. The crowd went berserk. The officer was wonderstruck.

The third time too Sadayappan came running at great speed. The crowd was absolutely convinced that this time the stone would reach the other side of the pond. And—it did. No one could see where the stone fell. One of the men who had been appointed to keep a watch on the game lifted a stone from the ground and shouted out to the crowd. Sadayappan was then lifted by the crowd in celebration. Many of the spectators were keen on finding out who he was and from which village. Suddenly, Aattur Sadayappan's name was on everyone's lips. Until then, no one had known him. He had stayed confined to his field. But within a few minutes, he had become famous.

The British officer was nonplussed at the development, but without showing it on the outside, he joined in the celebration. He got off the horse and shook Sadayappan's hands and patted him on the back, while Sadayappan stood hunched in deference. In front of the entire crowd, he was awarded the prize money of ten rupees. Kali's grandmother pointed out to the land where the barnyard now stood and told them that it was with those ten rupees that the land was bought.

There was no British officer next to the temple pond this time. That happened forty or fifty years ago, and many other officers came after him. Whenever anyone asked Sadayappan how he managed to do what no one else could, he said, 'I just prayed to god and flung the stone. It must have been them who made sure the stone fell where no one could see it.'

When Ponna wondered how he managed to do that, Kali's grandmother lowered her voice and said, 'I haven't told this to anyone. He is dead and gone, too. That British officer too is not around now, but it is the British who are still ruling. If they hear of it, they will lock us up in jail.' There was fear in her voice.

'I won't tell anyone, Grandma. Share it with me,' said Ponna.

Grandmother narrowed her eyes and said, 'If they come to know, they might rampage through our land, dear. Don't tell anyone.' She made Ponna promise before she shared the secret.

When Sadayappan walked around the pond, he made note of the fact that they did not allow anyone to hang out on the other side of the pond. There was just one man allowed there, who was supposed to observe where the stones fell. Sadayappan was certain that his throw would reach the stone at least three-quarters of the way. He decided that he would try a trick to get the stone to the other side. Well, if they found out, he would just get some extra whiplashes. Won't his robust body bear that much of an onslaught? he reasoned. He could have thrown the very first stone three-fourths of the distance, but he controlled himself and let it travel only half the way. This way, he could build up the next throw to three-quarters and gain people's confidence that he would eventually win. In fact, his third throw rested entirely on the strength of this confidence.

When he receded to the outer end of the east bank to start running for lead, he pretended to have dropped the stone. While bending down to look for it, he picked it up with his left hand, while his clenched fist just gave the impression of holding the stone. He then gently dropped the stone that was in his left hand and ran with his clenched right hand that appeared to be holding a stone. No one suspected anything. Everyone's attention was focused on seeing where the stone would fall in the pond. And since it did not fall anywhere inside the pond, they all concluded that it must have fallen on the other bank. The man on guard on the other side was scared that he would be chastised for slackening in his job, so he picked up a random stone and proclaimed, 'Here! This is where it fell.' This was the secret of Sadayappan's victory.

Ponna was shocked on hearing this. Was it right to make one's living through something that was earned by cheating? She even suspected that was the reason for their being childless. He might have been a British officer. He might have been a cruel man who dealt people whiplashes. Wouldn't the gods make sure he was punished adequately for that? Was it all right to cheat him and take ten rupees from him? Was it good for the family? Weren't there thousands of people around the pond that day? Didn't this mean the money was received by cheating everybody? It might have been a big achievement for him, but . . .

It wouldn't have mattered if he'd spent the money on some temple expenses. It would even have been all right if he'd wasted it away in food and drinks. Instead, he bought land and made sure the consequences of his action went down generations. That's why god had ensured there was no further heir. Ponna brooded over this for a few days. Since she didn't want to upset Grandmother at her age, she didn't say anything. But when she shared her concern with Kali, he laughed.

'Do you think no one would have known if he had no stone in his hand and just made a gesture of throwing it? Do you think that British officer was an idiot? The stone that my grandfather threw would definitely have reached the other side. Do you think he was an ordinary man? He might have been short, but he was very strong. Don't worry about this,' he said.

She insisted that they should sell the land and spend the money on rituals. She said whatever land would be left after that would suffice. He was not at all in agreement with her about selling the land. Which farmer would so easily agree to let go of his land?

'If you think this is definitely the reason, we could go ahead and do it just for the sake of a child. But I don't believe it is so. I say this for you,' he said.

Soon after, Ponna took her mother-in-law along, took a bath in the temple pond and went to the base of the hill and made an offering. When Kali's grandmother was on her deathbed, she asked her: 'Are we suffering the consequences of that, Paatti?'

With tears in her eyes, Kali's grandmother said, 'We prayed to god, consulted him with flowers and bought this land with his blessing, dear one. So, nothing will happen because of that.'

Only after that did Ponna feel a bit consoled. She was determined to complete her offering as soon as a child was born.

Now, they moved beyond the pond and towards the bungalows. There were small stalls lining the road. People could buy rice puffs and mochai seeds and eat as they walked along. The smell of jaggery attracted them. 'Shall we buy something?' said her mother, but Ponna was not interested in anything. They walked past the crowds from one street to the next. There was a big market under way there. It had plenty of bangle shops. Her mother compelled Ponna and made her wear some new bangles. She also bought some hairpins. Ponna stood there as if she was somehow disconnected from all of it.

When they turned to the east, they saw brilliant lights. In the light of the moon above, the big chariot appeared magnificent. It looked like its sharp roof could pierce the skies. Though the chariot had reached its spot after making its rounds, its giant ropes still lay on the street. People were touching the rope in prayer. That entire street was full of steel merchandise: cast-iron work, spades, dosai pans, sickles and other such stuff. There were crowds in front of every shop. She could hear voices bargaining. When she got up after bending down to touch the large iron chain that lay in the middle of the road like a large serpent, she couldn't find her mother.

twenty-nine

As soon as he gulped down a small pitcher of coconut toddy, his tummy cooled down. It had a sweet–sour taste. Kali then stuffed his mouth with a handful of mochai seeds. Muthu and Mandayan sat opposite him. Katthayi lay inside the hut. Both the children were asleep, but Katthayi was still awake and listening to the voices outside in case they might call her suddenly. Though she had kept everything ready for them, they might suddenly ask her to help with something. The string-bean dish she had made with sesame and chilli powder was still inside. She had roasted some eggplant and made a gravy dish. Everything was untouched. She was worried about how much of it would be left over.

It always happened this way. They would initially plan to eat a lot after drinking. But they fell down flat after eating just a little bit. From a very young age, she had seen this happening to many men. Her mother was much smarter than her. She always made only half of what the men asked her to cook. Katthayi still hadn't found the courage to do that. What if it was not enough? What would she do? Mandayan would give her a thrashing with the coconut stem. He might look like a little fat insect, but his hands were like whips. Well, there will be enough food for tomorrow. Let the children eat rice for a change. They only got to eat kambu millets and porridge otherwise. If she kept the rice pot on top of the water pot and closed it properly, it wouldn't get spoilt. Even if she killed a chicken and made some gravy the next day, this rice would be enough.

She'd almost asked Kali if he had children, when she stopped herself. What if it made him sad? After coming to this grove, she hadn't cooked this kind of food for anyone else. Muthu was like a brother to her; he was a good man. He came once in a while and always spoke to her kindly. She had agreed to make all this food because it was for him. It was just as well, because she didn't know Kali too would come.

She could hear their conversation very clearly. She hoped to hear something about a child. The moment she heard Mandayan's voice, she stepped out with the string-bean dish she had made. There were enough mochai seeds in the bowl. Kali ate a mouthful of the string beans and said, 'Tastes like intestine curry.' It made Katthayi very happy.

'Is Ponna akka well?' she asked hesitantly.

'Hmm. Why wouldn't she be? She's well,' he said.

She didn't know what else to say. But feeling that she had to say something, she said, 'Shall I bring the rice and gravy?'

Ponna used to talk sweetly to Katthayi. Since she was a new wife when she went to their village, Katthayi was quite clueless and couldn't have lasted there even for a year but for Ponna's support. She prayed quietly that only good things should have befallen Ponna akka.

It looked like Muthu too was drinking slowly that day. The moon cast its light well on the spot where they were sitting. Mandayan refilled the pitchers with toddy from the barrel. It had been years since Kali had drunk coconut toddy. Once, Muthu had fetched a dried-gourd container filled with the toddy. Kali and Ponna were visiting then. Muthu took Kali into the fields. It was the season before the harvest, so the kambu crops were as tall as human beings. Since it had rained very well, it was wet and cold among the plants. Muthu walked into the fields softly without leaving footprints. It was very difficult for Kali to do the same.

In the middle of the millet field, there was a rock large enough to build a cattle enclosure on. Muthu had built a tiny hut on top of it. It looked like a hen coop. It was not very high; one had to crawl to get into it and sit down. No one looking at the field from outside would even know there was a hut in the middle of it. He had used tender palm leaves to weave the hut without any holes on its surface. So, he could lie there on rainy days too. Now he made a fire outside the hut using some dry twigs that didn't give out much smoke. Then he fried some eggs. That was the last time Kali had had any coconut toddy.

'Muthanna, I didn't know our landlord was your brother-in-law,' said Mandayan. 'Had I known, I'd have invited him long ago. It is always a delight to see him drink toddy. It makes me want to keep pouring him more. Most men would drink it all in a gulp and keep spitting here and there.'

Muthu laughed, 'Mandaya! You are referring to me, aren't you?'

'Oh, not you, brother! You don't keep spitting,' said Mandayan and kept a bottle of arrack before him. 'It was brewed yesterday. Do try it.'

'Mandaya, do you brew this often?'

'No, samee, if I set aside what is left of the toddy, I can brew some arrack every fifteen days or so. The owner of this grove prefers only arrack. Also, when the Muslim merchant—the one who owns this place—comes, he always carries a bottle with him. We are lacking in nothing here, brother. After having come here, we are finally making some money. We have been able to stay put in one place without wandering around with all our stuff.'

'It looks like your wife doesn't like the place that much.'

'Oh, don't bother about her. What better place can a tree climber expect to be in? Her worry is that if we fall sick, we don't have any relatives to ask after us. Well, even if they are nearby, do relatives always care for us? It is the problem of children that worries me most. We roam around here and there. But we can't just drink toddy and hang around as we wish. We have two children who look like little sheep. Now she has conceived again. The first two are still so small, and now another is on the way. We don't know how we're going to manage.'

'Why don't you get it aborted?'

'She is scared of it. In our village, a girl died after they inserted a plant stem to abort her foetus. Since then, we're scared to think of that option. If she dies, how will I raise these two? And even if we have four more, won't they somehow grow up if I just feed them some toddy?'

Kali's head reeled as soon as he drank the arrack from the pitcher. Arrack made from coconut toddy had a distinct taste.

'All right, don't worry. Just give me the child that is going to be born. I will raise it,' Kali said to Mandayan.

Muthu was relieved to see Kali gulp down more of the toddy. He knew they would have to spend the night there. Even if they left at dawn, the people who'd gone to the festival would have returned before they reached.

'Samee, don't you have a child yet?'

'Don't get me started on that. There is nowhere we have not prayed, no god we have not made offerings to. Nothing has happened, Mandaya. That's why I'm asking you for your child.'

'That's it, then. I will give you the child that is going to be born. You raise it.'

Katthayi rushed out of the hut in anger and said to her husband, 'Will you eat shit when you are drunk? You have promised him now. What will you do if he comes for real later and asks for the child? How can we just give away a child we have given birth to? Even if we do, how can our child grow up in his household? Think before you speak! If they heard us, his relatives will come here to beat us to pulp. Let him find a child from among his relatives.'

'So, you won't give it to me?' said Kali. 'Give it! I will take care of the child. I will also see which fucker objects . . .' And Kali slid down on the mat. Remembering that he hadn't eaten anything, Muthu asked Katthayi to bring some food. Then he mashed it well and fed Kali. But Kali just said, 'I want a child . . . a child . . .' and fell back again on the mat. While Muthu and Mandayan were eating, Kali's drunken rant continued.

Let him empty out his mind, thought Muthu. Just a question about a child had upset him so much. Muthu felt very sorry for him.

thirty

Ponna found herself standing alone in the middle of a large crowd. She couldn't find her mother anywhere. Though there were faces milling around everywhere, none of them were familiar to her. Where did her mother go? Her supportive hand had been on Ponna's shoulders all this while. She must have mingled with the crowd when Ponna's eyes were glued to the top of the large chariot. She might have wandered off when Ponna was busy looking at the shops with ironware suited for any kind of work. In that one unknown moment, when her eyes were lost in the spectacle of things, everything known to her must have taken leave of her.

For a little while, she stood frozen in fear, but the crowd eventually pushed her in one direction or another. She drifted along like a piece of wood in a flood. The large lanterns hanging in the streets were heaving like snakes. The men who were rekindling fading lanterns stood out in the crowd. Policemen too were wandering the streets armed with lathis. She observed the dark shadows and dots of light casting themselves on the crowd, making everyone look like objects of smoke. She recognized none of the faces. It amazed her that there were so many people in this town. How many must there be in this entire world! The earth seemed to hold innumerable people, but none of them were known to her.

She looked around for anyone she knew from the village. No one. Any relatives? Anyone she had worked with in the fields? From within her mind, she brought out several faces that she had known since childhood and checked to see if any of the faces in the crowd now matched any of those from her mind's inventory. None. Even if any face matched, it might not mean anything. Once people enter such a large crowd, everyone becomes a new, unknown face. Mine has become a new face too. Has my mother made me new by making me wear flowers and glass bangles? Do they change everything? It was the job of mothers everywhere to make things new, and to do this, they made themselves anew too. Here, my face, my body, my appearance—everything has become new. Isn't this what I need to become a mother?

I need to fear only if I am among known faces and in known places. I'd have to be scared about what might happen, what people might say. Have I ever been able to do anything just the way I have desired to? There has always been the fear that someone familiar might chance upon me. Everyone is here. And also no one. She was overcome with a huge sense of relief. Once her fear abated, she saw everything with fresh eyes. Everything was new to her. When she realized how attracted she was by the glamour of newness, she saw that she was standing next to the wheel of the chariot.

She felt that, just like the wheel of the chariot, she had abandoned what she was accustomed to and was standing firmly in what was new. She had a sudden desire to run and jump amidst the crowd. She wanted to explode into laughter. There was nothing to stop her here. She could do anything she wanted to. She yearned to see the entire town in one long run. But she should control herself. She thought she could absorb nothing if she lost her balance.

There were four paths ahead of her. To the west of the chariot was the eighty-pillared hall. Once she went past the eighty-pillared hall, she could see the temple at the foothills, looking as if it was standing with its arms outstretched. Around this were the temple streets. These then branched into different streets and led to the various roads. Good lord! How many paths she could take! On the streets branching off the ones bordering the temple, there were several halls where dance and music performances were taking place. From where she stood, she could hear them faintly.

The east street had two exits, one each on its north and south ends. And midway between these, there was a performance going on. To the east of the chariot was another street that ran straight to the base of the hill and then around it. She could not decide which path to take. But she was delighted at the sheer number of options she had! Without jumping to a decision immediately, she savoured that happiness of simply having options.

Then, involuntarily, she walked southward. Did her feet choose this direction because it was the most crowded there?

Was it the crowd that was guiding her? When she walked past the smaller chariots that had been stationed in a row, she saw that a dance event was in progress at the junction of four streets. In a space surrounded by flame torches, more than ten young men were dancing with sticks in their hands. From the centre of the wide space cleared in the middle of the crowd, which was now standing in a circle, she heard the sound of sticks clashing against one another—a perfectly coordinated, disciplined sound. Some of the people in the first row of the circle were seated. All the young men dancing had tied their topknots in the same style. When they leapt up in the air, their dhotis, which they had fastened by bringing the cloth from between their legs and tucking it in at the back, appeared to loosen. Ponna wondered what sort of knot was holding the dhotis in place.

There weren't many women in the crowd. She could see only some old women and little girls sitting about. Among those standing around the dancers, all she found were a few women dotting the crowd like stones in a plate of rice. They were standing right behind those who were seated, the best place to see the dance from. Ponna felt that she could watch forever the way the topknots of the dancing men bounced up and fell back on their napes; each of the men had tightly combed back his hair, fastening it into a knot at the nape. She liked the way they worked their sticks, sometimes separated as two teams, and at other times as one, but always leaving enough space for the sticks to clash, always doing it without the least discordance. It felt like the clank of the sticks was hitting open the knots in her mind. This dance was not just about sticks clashing. It was not just mere combat. It was the play of magic wands which cracked open facades to bring out hidden secrets.

She shut her eyes. When she opened them, she saw bodies glistening with sweat and lit by the flame torches. All the bodies looked alike—like black rocks that had been set upright and carved into bodies. The tightening and relaxing of the muscles on these bodies made her mind swing back and forth. The earrings that the men wore glowed in the light. The sound of their ankle bells matched perfectly the sound of the sticks. They all looked like gods. They paused in between movements. She wondered if she should just remain there. But there would be much more to see in all the other streets.

While she was thinking about this, she felt a touch on her right arm. She was not able to turn around immediately. She felt a lack of desire in that touch. Kali's embrace was like this sometimes; his mind would be far from her, hovering somewhere else. It was merely the body working. It panicked her that thoughts of Kali should choose this moment to arrive. What brought up these old things? But then, was it easy to shake off the things that lay layered on top of each other in her mind? It was no problem casting aside superficial concerns. But there were those that had seeped deep into the mind, and lay there rotting. Was it an easy task to hack at them and throw them out?

To avoid thinking about Kali, she turned to look at the face of whoever had grabbed her arm. He was ready with a smile, a smile that he had prepared to meet her with, whenever she turned around. He was young, but the smile was not the kind that showed an interest for the experience. Instead, it betrayed an arrogance that was simply interested in increasing the number of his exploits. He was no god. Her mother had said every man was a god that night. Perhaps. But Ponna was clear he was not the god meant for her. She jerked his hand off and moved away. She did not turn to look at him again. Though she was overcome with an urge to leave the place right away, she decided to stay put for a while.

Now the sounds of the sticks refused to register in her mind. The sounds of the ankle bells and those of the sticks came separately to her. And the figures seemed to move in a way completely disconnected with the sounds. She pulled each figure away from the crowd. She embraced and kissed each one of them. When she felt that that was all she had to offer to those gods, she left the place and mingled with the crowd in the south street. She didn't know what it led to. Anyway, it was better if she found out once she reached there. She had done enough of walking towards the known and the familiar. At least on this one night, she wanted to make full use of the opportunity to walk towards the new and the unknown.

On the lane that branched off from the south street and went towards the temple at the base of the hill, the crowd was standing in a circle. She rose to her toes to take a look at what was going on. It was a Karagattam performance, the dance where people balanced decorated metal pots on their heads.

There were four dancers—two men and two women. But were they really women or were they men dressed as women? She couldn't tell, despite looking at them closely. They were at the end of a movement where they danced bouncing up and down in keeping with the sound of the naayanam. She was tired of seeing it every year at the Mariamman temple festival. So her feet took her away from the spot. Looking at the moving crowd, she wondered if, like her, everyone else too was wandering alone. There were all kinds of people there: those walking alone, two people walking together, and people walking in fives and sixes making a lot of noise. They were all mostly men.

There were so few women in the crowds that Ponna could count them on the fingers of her hand. Perhaps they were all huddled close to the shops. The women were interested in buying something or the other. The shops would remain there right until the month of Aadi. She could come sometime later with Kali. But then how much stuff did two people need? The stuff she had brought as dowry still lay in the loft, covered in cloth. If they had a toddler, they could buy little wooden toys, dolls carved of wood, this and that. But now all they needed was some farm instrument made of iron.

A group walking behind her was full of laughter and revelry. She turned around just a little. They were teenagers. She felt that they might pounce on her even if she paused at the spot for a little while. How would she recognize her god in this group? As they neared her, she could smell the arrack on their breath.

'Oh, this will endure everything, da. A young tree. Shall we climb it?'

'Sure. You take the top, I will take the bottom.'

The language of groups was distasteful too. To protect herself from the disgust that their words induced in her, she walked away fast. The Poovayi temple was at the junction of the south and west streets. A play was being performed in the wide grounds behind the temple. She could hear a song floating in from there, sounding like a voice from deep within a well.

Oh Ganapathi, the one born before Kandan, lead my way
I hold your feet, protect me

She suspected that the group was still following her. She ran towards the grounds. Every year now, she had come to the Poovayi temple to offer pongal. It was also traditional at this temple to walk on a bed of fire in gratitude for prayers answered. She had vowed to do that if her prayers were answered and she conceived a child. The temple was just a thatched hut, and people were entering the grounds by walking in from either side. It was only after she followed the crowd and entered the grounds that she felt a little better. What if the men had managed to trap her? She reasoned that something like that could not happen in festival times with so many people around. She took her mind away from those thoughts and focused on the play.

thirty-one

The play had just begun, and there wasn't much of a crowd yet. They would start coming in now. But considering there was so much going on in all the streets, this was an impressive crowd, the kind of crowd that sits down and watches something. The clown was singing the welcome song:

Welcome! Welcome! Welcome!
Come, sit down, sit down, sit down!

He came around on all sides and exhorted everyone to 'Sit down, sit down.' But it looked like many people had planned to watch for a while and then move on. So, very few people obliged the clown.

Then he dragged on, 'Appanmaare! Annanmaare! Fathers! Brothers!' But the harmonium player stopped playing, looked at the clown and said, 'You babbling idiot! Can't you speak sensibly? Since when do appan and annan have breasts?' He was clearly punning on the word 'maar' that the clown had used simply as a plural suffix, but which also referred to breasts. Everyone laughed.

But the clown was up to the repartee. He said, 'Ah, the times have come to this! You are good at playing the box, but you can't speak a word properly. And you call me a babbler? You are a babbler, you father's a babbler, your mother and wife are babblers. Also, don't you frequent a woman in the devadasi quarters? She's a babbler, too!' The crowd laughed at his layered attack.

The harmonium player beat a retreat, saying, 'Good lord! You are the god of words. You definitely speak meaningfully.'

'All right, I will sing sensibly as you asked me. Listen,' said the clown.

Older sisters, younger sisters,
Mothers and grandmothers,
Redden your tongue
With betel leaves and nuts
And come, sit down, sit down!

But he continued to use 'maar' as the plural form, enunciating it extra clearly, and emphasized the double entendre by heaving his chest up and down as he finished the song.

Ponna walked past the people sitting on the mats that were normally used as partitions. She wanted to sit right in the front. As she waded through the crowd, light from the flame torches suddenly illuminated her. She tightened her sari around her torso and continued walking, when the clown pointed at her and said: 'Aha! Look who has come! Kumari Rukmini amma herself, who played the role of Valli, Lord Murugan's consort from the movie *Sri Valli* has come from Chennapattanam to watch our play! What style! What beauty! How glamorously has she tied her sari! What gait! What a dancer! O peacock, won't you be my messenger . . . Everyone! Please put your hands together and give her a place to sit.'

Everyone looked at Ponna, clapped and laughed. Then the clown started singing a famous song from the movie *Sri Valli*: 'In the forest that never dries up . . .' Everyone's attention was fully on Ponna. When she realized it was her that the clown had referred to as the actress Kumari Rukmini, she was overcome with shyness. She dropped her chin and quickly sat down where she could find a spot.

Kali had taken her to watch some movies. The movie *Sri Valli* had run at Kannan Talkies for several days. All the village folk arranged bullock carts and went in large groups to watch it. 'Oh, it is the story of our Pazhani Murugan,' was what everyone kept saying.

Her mother-in-law, however, was not pleased with the idea. She went on and on: 'I have never seen a farmer who went to strange parts of town in the middle of the night to watch a play. And what I cannot believe is that this girl too wants to go along! As if that wasn't enough, now they are showing a film, it seems, and these two are going for that!'

Kali said, 'Amma, shut up. This is a movie about our god Pazhani Murugan. Everyone's going. You come too, if you want.'

'Of course!' she snapped sarcastically. 'Am I at an age to go and see people dropping their clothes and prancing around? You two get lost.'

Kali and Ponna went to watch the movie. They walked along with a crowd that looked as big as the one that went every year on Panguni Utthiram carrying kavadis to Pazhani. Ponna did not understand the film much, so Kali kept explaining it to her now and then. He was used to coming with his friends to watch films at night. But Ponna had only seen three or four films, so she had difficulty understanding certain things. She could not make sense of the lyrics. She felt sleepy after a while. But, despite all these constraints, they managed to watch *Sri Valli*. She thought that the actress Rukmini who played Valli was extremely beautiful. Her unblemished face had stayed in Ponna's mind. She even touched her cheek, wondering if she would ever be as beautiful as Rukmini. Perhaps if she wore a blouse and jewellery like she did. As she wondered how she'd look with a blouse on, she pulled her sari to cover her chest properly.

She felt bad that the clown had made her the butt of ridicule. But then she took comfort in the fact that no one was looking at her any more. It was only after she sat down that she realized she had walked and run a long distance. Her legs begged for some rest.

In the part of the village where the farmhands lived, there

was always a play when there was a temple festival. In the month of Thai, there was another ceremony, and they had performed plays then too. But it happened in the cremation ground, so the others did not go for that. For the one that happened during the temple festival, the farm labourers kept a separate spot for the farm owners to watch the play from. Ponna had seen many such performances. The clown could make even the most morose of people laugh. Hoping that she would find some solace if she let her mind enter the play, she started paying attention.

A man, who was not in costume, came to announce what the play was about in a pompous speech: 'The fact of the matter is, the eighteenth day of the festival is going on with aplomb in Karattur, which is such a heaven on earth and is so fertile with gold, dairy and paddy that the crores of celestial beings and even the three gods—Brahma, Vishnu and Shiva—along with their consorts are considering staying on here! The god and goddess of the hill—who are variously called Mangaipangan, the half-female god, Maadhorubaagan, the one who is one part woman, and Ammaiyappan, the mother–father god—came down from the hill, went around the four main streets in procession, blessed various villages with their presence, and today they are about to go back to the hill . . .'

The clown had to rupture all this bombast! He said, 'This man says the god and goddess roamed around the villages. But are they jobless like you? Wherever they roam about, they have to come back here eventually. That's why we have this eighteenth day of the festival. All right, what was it you said about Ammaithazhumbu, the chickenpox scar?'

The announcer was ready to handle this pun on words. 'Not Ammaithazhumbu, pa. I said Ammaiyappan, the mother–father form.'

The clown, who was on a roll by now, replied, 'Oh, you mean your mother and your father? Okay. Didn't you say something else? Something about Madhiyaanasoru, the afternoon meal? You were mentioning that you and I didn't eat lunch, weren't you?

The announcer was exasperated: 'Ayyo! Not that, pa.'

The clown now pretended to take offence to his being addressed as 'pa', which was both a respectful, endearing way to address someone as well as a short form for 'appa'. 'Stop! Why do you keep addressing me as "pa"? How did I become you father? I don't even know who your mother is. Are you trying to grab a share of my wealth?'

Announcer: 'Well, what wealth do you have, pa?'

Clown: 'See! You are calling me "pa" again!'

The announcer had had it. He switched to the much less respectful 'da', and said, 'All right, you useless motherfucker. Tell me how much wealth you got.'

'Good, now that's a more respectable way to address me. I have five acres next to the river and seven acres next to the lake. But I'm not going to give them to anyone. Even when I die, they will remain in my name. Now you come back to the matter at hand. What were you saying about Madhiyaanasoru, our lunch?' said the clown.

'No one wants your land. Keep it, da. I was not talking about Madhiyaanasoru but about Maadhorubaagan, the one who is one part female. The god who stands on the Karattur hill and has the goddess for his left half. That is why he is called Maadhorubaagan. Do you understand, da?'

The clown switched to mock anger now, and said, 'Hey! What is this? You are using the "da" too often now!' Then he lamented his bad fate: 'Why should I have to struggle with this disrespectful man! All right. So, Madhiyaanasoru means to be half male and half female? So they stay right next to each other? But what's the use if they can't touch each other?'

The announcer was now disgusted at these sacrilegious remarks. 'Chee!' he said. 'Don't say such dirty things on this auspicious day. You will land up in hell for the next seven births.'

'Oh! So you think you will go to the glorious heaven?' retorted the clown. 'When you die, no one will even volunteer to decorate your hearse. People come only when you have amassed some wealth. You have nothing.'

Then he turned to the audience, and continued, 'In the morning, you will see him buying some puttu on credit from the poor woman.'

Back to addressing the announcer, the clown said, 'What uncouth thing did I say? I said the male and female sides cannot touch each other despite being so close. What's wrong with that? You and I came about because they touched, isn't it? You call this dirty?'

215

Either out of sheer exasperation or because the play had to begin at some point, the announcer broke into an invocation song seeking the blessings of Ganapathi before beginning the play based on the well-known story of Siruthondan, a devotee of Lord Shiva.

'The play that we are going to present today is the story of the King of Kanchi—the most fertile and prosperous of kingdoms. He did great service to the devotees of our Lord by offering them food every day. One day, the Lord tested him by asking the King to give him his own son, the prince. And the King did. The Lord then brought the King's dear son back to life. If those without children are watching this play, they will be blessed with a child . . .'

Here the clown cut in and took over, 'Those without husbands will be blessed with husbands and those who do not have wives will be blessed with wives. Isn't that so?'

The crowd doubled up in laughter. No one had left the audience. In fact, some more people had joined in. Ponna felt that the clown was the strength of this troupe. He was definitely going to hold the audience's attention till the end. But she did not like the fact that they were playing Siruthondar's story. She had seen it once in the other festival, in the farmhand quarters. Since someone had prayed for a child and got one, they had arranged for the play to be performed. And several people from that part of town came one after the other to invite Ponna. When the moment came in the play wherein the prince Seeralan is killed for food, there was not a dry eye in the audience.

Ponna remembered how heart-rending it was when the musicians sang about how the king sharpened his knife before killing his own son for the offering. She remembered the song describing how he sharpened his knife on sandalwood and then on a vermilion slab. When they sang, 'As the mother held the son's hands and feet, the father slit his throat,' she heard many women sobbing away in the audience. When the ordeal was over and Seeralan was brought back to life, the custom was to wave two lemons around him in a circle. No matter how many people came with lemons, their lemons were circled around the person who played Seeralan and given back. Women who received a lemon in their laps were blessed with children. Ponna too received a lemon in her lap. She did that every time the Punnadayan story was sung in the village. But nothing happened.

Well, it is only from those whom he has blessed with a child that the Lord can demand such an offering. What would you ask, oh Lord, from those who don't have children?

She wanted to leave from there.

thirty-two

At that moment, someone came and sat rubbing against her. In her head, she tried to classify the nature of that graze. But she couldn't. Was this her god? She glanced slowly at the man who was rubbing and pressing down on her right shoulder. She saw an eager face with a thin moustache. His eyes looked directly into hers. She felt she had seen those eyes somewhere, but she could not remember where and when. She closed her eyes and searched her mind. By then he had sat down comfortably, huddling against her, and was trying to rest his face on her shoulder. She could not decide whether to allow it or not, but she knew she had to make up her mind before it proceeded any further. She shifted her body gently and suggested her disapproval. But she did it in a way that did not mean rejection either. It made her wonder when she had become so clever. Perhaps she had always been so. Perhaps it was finding expression only now.

Kali was adept at reading the nuances of her movements. Even if he sensed a slight rejection, he would move away immediately. At those times, it would become very hard for her to get him interested again. She jerked her head to get Kali off her mind, and his image receded and vanished. She turned and looked. The eyes and the face she saw nudged a memory—it was as though a bolt of lightning flashed across her face, and for a moment she thought she recognized him. But it was not him; only a likeness. Ponna came of age when she was fourteen. And the face that had been in her mind then was Sakthi's. He had been a goatherd in their farm for many years, and she had grown up playing with him. Later, when she was a young woman, his had been the face of her dreams and her imagination. When it was decided that Kali would marry her, she had struggled a lot to replace Sakthi in her mind with Kali.

Whatever she started imagining with Kali in her mind would end up with Sakthi's face being part of the fantasy. For some time, she even vacillated between the two faces. But after the wedding, Sakthi's face slowly faded away and over time she even forgot him completely. But here it was again, and so close to her. Suddenly, she decided she did not want him. She moved away a little and avoided the intimacy. But his heavy sigh wafted in the air and bothered her. When she turned around, his eyes were pleading with her, and his arms were stretched out towards her. She felt like laughing, but she showed him an angry face, shook her head in refusal, and turned her back to him. How easily he asked for what he wanted even in the middle of such a crowd! It amazed her that she could conduct an entire conversation with him without anyone noticing. It was only then that she grew conscious of her surroundings. She looked around and dropped her head shyly.

On stage, Siruthondar had entered in a dance movement and was introducing himself. It looked like the dance performance might actually be good. She looked towards the man through the corner of her eye. He wasn't there. She thought she would leave too. But that might give him the idea that she had come out looking for him. It might be good to leave after a while. The things this god did! He dug out a forgotten face from the depths of her heart and placed it in front of her. Was it her punishment to remember that face forever? 'Please appear with a new face, one I am not familiar with,' she prayed. Had she earned his wrath after having rejected two of the gods? Is this a crowd of gods too? Is he watching me?

It looked like there was a way leading out in every direction; there were gods wandering everywhere. 'Come to me with a form I like,' she kept praying. She went past the Poovayi temple and reached the west street. There was a wide space at the intersection with the north street. Hearing some loud whistling from there, she walked in that direction. She was thirsty. Was it her mind's thirst that was peeping out through her tongue? On the west street, there were four or five unmanned water pandals. Anyone could help themselves to the water. She drank some and splashed some cold water on her face. She felt refreshed.

She glanced at the temple. In the moonlight, its tower looked taller. When she reached the crowded street corner, all the while praying in her mind, she saw a team of Oyilattam dancers performing there. There were over twenty of them; they all wore yellow headbands and held long red streams of cloth in their hands and danced in rhythm to the drums. She looked in amazement at how, when they took four steps in unison and turned around suddenly, the several pieces of coloured cloth that waved in the air flared and settled like snakes flying in the air with their tongues out. She was familiar with the dance. This was the same dance that was performed on all nine days of the Mariamman temple festival. Youngsters trained in summer with a teacher. Also, because it was done in the temple, it was called Koyilattam. It started with a slow movement of the hands and feet, but it gradually gained speed and reached a crescendo. And as the dance grew faster, the whistles grew louder. Sometimes, the performance opened with a song and every dance was alternated with a song. But this dance looked different, perhaps because of the colours that had been added to it.

Whenever she heard the whistles, she was beside herself, clapping and jumping in joyful laughter. It looked like she might even join the dancers. The beauty of it, when they moved to the front and turned around, was so intense that it wrapped itself around everything in the vicinity. Looking at the dancers, she wondered if men were really such beautiful creatures. She felt a wild urge to run and embrace them. She jumped and almost fell on the girl standing next to her. But the girl didn't take it amiss; she just laughed. 'I don't see women performing anywhere,' she said in a gossipy tone. It looked like she too would have liked to join them. Ponna gave her a friendly smile.

When she felt something touching her earlobes, she reached back and wiped herself. It felt as though someone was blowing gently on her nape. She turned around and saw a pair of eyes to her side. She knew it was the touch of these eyes that had bothered her. Those eyes pierced the glow of the burning torches, and touched and teased her. The folded dhoti and the towel that was around his neck and fell over his chest made him look like no one she knew. His hair had been combed carelessly, and it looked like he had not even started shaving. It occurred to her that this was her god. His eyes smiled. His lips too were parted in a permanent grin. In a delightful, repetitive game, his eyes moved towards the dance only to turn back to her suddenly. She looked fondly at that desire-filled face. Then she closed her eyes and tried holding it in her mind. But it slipped away. She could recollect the eyes, the lips and the head separately, but she could not put them together. Why wouldn't it stay in her mind?

It was unlike any other face that had stayed on in her mind. It was never easy for a new face to make its place in a shelf of faces. 'This is how I expected you to be, god,' she thought. Then his eyelashes lowered and eyebrows slanted. She understood that he wanted her to walk out with him. She was overcome with shyness. When she remembered that Kali too often spoke this way—in signs—her mind closed up. She was never able to keep Kali aside. In twelve years, he had gradually etched himself on every fold of her heart. No one could do anything to him. She would find him in any man. She could recognize him in anyone. She felt like screaming at this image, pleading with him not to remind her of Kali. If she spoke to him in signs, he would respond like Kali too. She knew she had to leave from there and get to a place where they could talk in words.

When she emerged, parting her way through the crowd gathered around the Oyilattam troupe, he too came and joined hands with her. She was surprised that he read her mind so quickly. She felt that just a small shift of the body was enough for a man to understand a woman. The grip of his hand was comforting. He walked with her along the north street. She decided to let him lead. Along the way were shops selling puttu laid out on baskets layered with white cloth. There were small crowds here and there. His lips grazed her ears when they said, 'Shall we eat puttu?' A male voice dripping desire and intoxication. She didn't even think. She nodded. He peeped into every store, but didn't stop at any.

Finally, he stopped at a shop that was halfway down the street and got hot puttu on a leaf plate covered with dry leaves stitched together. There were four portions of puttu with gravy on the side. Though she thought she might not be able to eat so much, she did not refuse. He brought his plate and ate standing next to her. She liked the way he carefully chose the puttu after considering several shops. It made her happy to think that he would have chosen her the same way.

She took some puttu and put it on his plate, but she was too shy to look up at this face. 'Why? Enough already?' he said.

'Please speak some more,' she pleaded in her mind. With a man, that was how she always felt—like he did not speak enough. You want your dear one to talk to you non-stop.

She was eating, her head bent low, when he said, 'Selvi, look here.' When she looked up in shock, wondering who Selvi was, he brought a handful of puttu close to her lips. She let him feed her. 'He has given me a new name so that no one around here gets suspicious.' She found this cleverness very attractive. He continued to feed her without any hesitation. But her diffidence came in the way of her desire to reciprocate. As if he sensed that, he said, 'Hmmm,' and, bending close to her, held her hand and brought it to his lips. She fed him without looking up.

When they started walking again, she literally stuck to him. She did not know the way, and she had no sense of the people around her. 'He is my god. My job is to go where he takes me,' was all she could think. Like a rain-soaked chicken, she huddled in his warmth. It appeared that he was taking her far away from the crowds and the noise.

thirty-three

Kali woke up at exactly the same time he was used to for feeding the cows every night, but he could not rise because of an overpowering dizziness. He lay down for a little longer, tossing his head from side to side. The thatched mat he was lying on made crunching sounds under his head. When he sat up with some difficulty, he could see everything very clearly in the moonlight. The realization about where he was and in what circumstances dawned on him with a sharp pain. Suddenly, a roaring wind entered the coconut grove and pushed the fronds around. They made a great noise and it seemed that they were beating their chests. For a moment, Kali experienced great fear.

He was used to the sound of palm fronds rustling in the wind. They'd look like they were clutching their hands to their chests. But this was the first time he was witnessing how the coconut fronds spread their arms out and wailed in panic. Slowly, the wind died down. Outside the hut, Muthu and Mandayan were lying on mats that were facing different directions. All that great wind did nothing to disturb their sleep. When Kali got drunk and passed out, Muthu had been quite stable, which was unusual. Normally, it was Muthu who gulped down his alcohol like water and went flat very soon. How did it all change that night?

Perhaps Kali could not control the excitement at seeing coconut toddy and arrack. But he had been happy. He had not planned to spend the night here, but it all ended up working out that way. Maybe Muthu was used to coming here, getting drunk and lying around. That was why he did not say anything. Kali looked at the sky. He could not find the moon, but its light fell continuously through the gaps in the grove. He got up and washed his face with the water in the pot. His breath stank and his saliva tasted foul. So he spat it out and rinsed his mouth. He removed his dhoti, which was coming undone anyway, and wiped his face with it. Then he tightened his loincloth and wore the dhoti over it. His towel was caught under Muthu's sleeping body. He tried to pull it free, but he had to move Muthu a little to get it out. Then he sat on the mat.

He didn't know what to do. He couldn't fall asleep again. He never could sleep once he woke up at the time when the cattle needed to be fed. He always just stayed awake gazing around. If there was moonlight, he would carry a pot and go to the well. The barnyard needed twenty pots of water every day. What did it matter when he got that work done?

Though he knew he could not fall asleep again, he lay down and stretched his legs. Again, a mighty wind swept into the grove. Kali thought that it was only here that he was actually able to see the wind. If the wind was so strong in Aani, one could imagine how forceful it would have been in Aadi. No one would stay in the grove with such a wind blowing around and the trees screaming constantly. Perhaps, if one was used to it, one could stay. After all, Mandayan could not vacate the hut and run elsewhere just for the month of Aadi.

Mandayan was still full of affection for Kali. He kept saying 'Our landlord.' He even said yes when Kali asked for the child. He wondered what gift Mandayan had that whenever he slept with his wife, he had a child. The gods seemed to keep giving to someone who kept saying 'Enough!' while the one who desperately wanted it was simply told to fuck off. Even if Mandayan agreed to give the child, Katthayi wouldn't agree. However dire the circumstances might be, no mother would gladly give away her child. Like she said, would it work out to raise his child in Kali's home?

He remembered that even Ponna had once said that if it came to adopting a child, she would prefer one from the same caste. 'But not from our relatives. They will talk as if they have given us a portion of their wealth, and we cannot raise the child with them watching. Even if the child had a minor cold and fever, they'd say we did not take good care of it. If you can find a child from some unknown place, I will consider raising it.'

Kali too was not that keen on adopting a child. Would that stop people from talking? They'd only say, 'He calls himself the father to someone else's child.' Would this make them invite Kali to weddings and funerals and give him pride of place at special gatherings? He would still be the impotent one. Ponna would still be the barren woman.

On a moonlit night like this one, when they were in the barnyard and Ponna lay with him on the cot, she had said, 'We don't need to raise someone else's child, maama. We won't be able to be as loving to it as we could be to our own child. If the child does something stupid, we would think, "Had he been our own child would he have done this?" And he might also think, "They wouldn't talk to me like this if I were their own child." We don't need all that. If we manage to conceive one of our own, well and good. If not, we will just be the way we are.'

Another time, however, she spoke differently. Since it had rained well, they had planted cotton. The plants had grown nice and robust. The old woman who was supposed to be grazing an entire herd of goats in a nearby field dozed off, letting her goats wander into Kali's cotton field. When Ponna ran from the barnyard, they were busy munching away at the lush cotton plants. And by the time she chased them all out, a sizeable portion of the plants had been reduced to leafless stalks.

'Who knows which man she went with, abandoning her goats? Let her come. I will scoop the life out of her!' Ponna kept yelling.

Finally, the old woman arrived, looking somewhat sheepish. Seeing her, Ponna shouted in rage.

'I just dozed off in the heat,' the woman said nonchalantly. 'Why are you making a big deal out of it?'

Ponna's anger peaked. 'I am making a big deal out of it? Come and take a look. They have damaged one square measure of the crop. How dare you say I am making a big deal out it!'

To shut her up, the woman had just one thing in her arsenal, and she used it: 'Why do you worry so much about an heirless property?'

Ponna was shocked. But she collected herself and responded, 'So what? Have you come as the child to eat off my property?'

She was quite hurt by what the old woman had said. Outraged, she walked back to the barnyard and said to Kali, 'I don't know what you will do and how. I want a child right away.' This was not a doll he could get immediately from the shop, was it? He tried to soothe her, but to no avail.

'Go somewhere and get me a child!' Ponna raged. 'I don't care even if it is from an untouchable woman. I don't care if you have to buy one for money. I don't want anyone to be able to say that this property of ours has no inheritor. Go now!' And Ponna physically pushed Kali out of the barnyard.

She was very angry. But where would he go? How would he get a child? He stood there for a little while and then peeped inside. She was lying on the thrash floor. It took him great effort to console her that day. The topic of adopting a child usually flared up like this now and then and got put out on its own. To reclaim her from the effect of these conversations, he had to go home at night from the barnyard for a few nights. His intense embraces accomplished what his gentle words could not. If she slowly loosened her body and showed some involvement, it meant she had emerged from her despair.

thirty-four

To this day, Kali found something very inviting in Ponna's speech and demeanour. He felt that it would've been nice if he had stayed with her and not come along with Muthu. Only Ponna's mother would be with her, and if he knocked on the door and asked for some water, she'd understand his intention. It was not too late even now; he could still go back. It would be a long time before dawn. Even if he walked really slowly, he could get there before the blackbirds started chirping. Thoughts of Ponna excited him. Even the great wind blowing in the grove failed to quench his body's thirst. He sat up. Muthu was fast asleep. Let him come in the morning after drinking some more toddy, he thought. At home, they'd serve chicken in the morning. Kali could always come back here, bringing some for Muthu. He decided to tell Mandayan and leave.

Bottles of arrack stood by Mandayan's sleeping head. One was half full and the other was untouched. Kali took the latter; it might come of use. The half-full bottle also attracted him. He drank a little from it and it hit his empty stomach with a sharp sting. He looked around and saw coconuts lying next to the hut. He broke them open with the sickle that was lying at the hut's entrance. They were good, fleshy coconuts. He ate the pulp of one, took another with him, and emerged out of the grove.

The moon had slid slightly down the sky to the west. He did not even think about the long distance he had to walk. Lying on the cot under the portia tree, Ponna was beckoning him with outstretched arms. The only part of the walk that was difficult was when he had to get down to the stream and climb up on to the other side, where it was dark since the moonlight came filtered through the dense bushes. When the wind started again, he could hear the wailing of coconut fronds from behind. Once he climbed up, he saw elevated fields stretching to a great distance. There was also the comforting presence of palm trees here and there. Memories of days when he had walked along the fields after watching street plays scrolled across his mind.

A big crowd of them would walk and run through the fields, scaring even the birds sleeping on the trees. The next day, people living in the shacks along the fields would inquire about the previous night's noises. All of these ended when he got married. Nallayyan used to say, 'If one can freely get the pleasure of a woman without getting married, who would want to get married?'

He was right in a way. Was it only pleasure that came with marriage? It gave one an heir to complete one's final rites and to inherit one's wealth. Can one abandon a corpse because one didn't know where the fellow was from? If there was no one to do the final rites, one had to run around and find someone who could do it. You would have to fall at his feet and beg him. There are even stories where somebody had to write off his wealth to someone else just so he would have someone to complete his death rites. There was nothing more ignominious than having to take care of the property of an heirless man. Imagine the physical fights that would break out over Nallayyan's property when he died.

A while back, when he had come to Kali's barnyard, Nallayyan had said, 'I will write my property in your name. There is no one more important to me.'

Kali said, 'Ah! You are such a tease! Here I am, wondering what to do with my wealth, and you are offering me yours!'

'You will give birth to one,' said Uncle. 'And even if you don't, it's not a problem. Enjoy it all as long as you can, and when you think your days are over, write it off to someone or the other. Are we going to pack all this land into a sack and carry it with us when we go?'

Once, Nallayyan came with a large dish that was half-filled with chicken meat. The meat had been cooked in its juices and fried well. He also had a bottle of arrack with him. That was a time when Kali had a lot of work in the fields. He had worked for four days and had put out all the raagi to dry. The work of clearing the field of raagi stems was going on. While he allowed other people to pick the grains, he wouldn't let anyone else cut the stem. If he started very early in the morning when the mist still lingered, he could finish working on over half an acre before the sun hit his forehead. Once the grains were picked, what did it matter if the field stood for a week with just the stems? But Kali wouldn't have it. He would even cut them at night, if there was moonlight. Ponna didn't approve of this. There were always rodents in a raagi field, and snakes came to catch the rodents. Why risk anything at night?

Kali had been very happy to see that Nallayyan had come bringing that feast. He had come at the right time, because Kali was very tired after all the work. He drank the arrack and took bites of the meat. It was a good chicken dish that had been made by adding just the right amount of green chilli.

'Uncle, looks like you have learned to make excellent chicken gravy and fry it!' said Kali.

'Oh, I can't do such things,' said Uncle. 'I can't sit still in one place even for a little while. Then where am I going to have the patience to cook and fry? My brothers' wives bring me these things.' And he laughed, adding, 'You keep saying we need an heir to what wealth we save, don't you? But what's the use of having a child? Even those parents who have four or five children have been left to take care of themselves. They all die alone. But I won't die that way. See, when you have children, it is the unspoken understanding that they are going to inherit whatever you leave behind. But in my case, no one knows what I will do with my stuff, where it will go. So everyone trips over each other wanting to take care of me. The other day, I said, just for the sake of it, that since I didn't know who was going to take care of me, I was planning to write my property off to the temples and then go to die in some monastery somewhere. Since then, I am sent a big portion of whatever is cooked in my brothers' homes! Today, they made meat in both houses, and the farm boy and I could not finish eating it all. So I brought it here thinking you might like it.'

Apparently, Nallayyan's sisters-in-law were vying with one another to take care of him. They were pampering him: 'Is the meat enough, maama?' or 'Shall I bring you more gravy?'

'Everything comes to where I am sitting,' Uncle continued. 'I don't have to move anywhere. Do people who have children get treated this way? Don't worry. In the future, you will get all this attention too.' Saying this, he cheered Kali up.

Whenever he was talking to Nallayyan, Kali forgot the pain of being childless and found an excitement about life. He even felt convinced it was good not to have children. But very soon some other small matter would come to the fore, tease him, rekindle his yearning for a child and laugh at his plight. Kali felt that however much Nallayyan rationalized it, his plight was not great either. Uncle might have met several women in the market. He might have enjoyed the pleasures of coitus several times. All this was fine if it was just once in a while. But wasn't it sad if the dog had to dip its tongue in the cattle's water pot every time it felt hungry?

For instance, could Uncle Nallayyan have ever experienced the kind of late-night urge that Kali was experiencing now, the one propelled by thoughts of Ponna's body? How many kinds of urges had he felt since morning! Could Uncle ever feel the certainty that he could go home and quench his yearning? It was Ponna who made Kali aware of the secret nuances of the body. Just a slight movement of her eyes made his body toss and struggle. Even without a touch, she could make his body hers. If she touched him, his body became the two-sided drum, the kind that was played during theatrical performances. When she touched him with just a finger, his body-drum reverberated with a certain sound. If she held him with a hand, it made another distinct sound. And when she held him with both her hands, his body completely lost its control. When her touches progressed, his body moved with the increasing intensity of a body responding to a drum's rise to a crescendo.

His mother might have given birth to him and raised him, but her control over him was limited. Nothing compared to the power his wife wielded over him. It was for Ponna that he left behind his circle of friends and relatives and confined himself to the barnyard. She said, 'I will go if you want me to.' That didn't mean, 'I will go.' It meant, 'I will do anything for you.' Giving up everything was the only price he had to pay to have her rest in the palm of his hand, to nestle in the hold of his fist. Thinking of her, his body acquired speed. Not minding the mild dizziness, he walked on.

Pathways that meandered through fields with no

farmsteads led the way for him. Even from a distance, he could see his portia tree shaped like an umbrella of shadows. The wind had died. The tree looked like darkness itself. Would she open the door if he just gently tapped on it like he did at home? Or would she have gone to sleep after expecting him all night? On nights when he failed her expectation to go to her, she stayed awake. In the morning, she would burn him with her anger. The frenzy of her agitated body was too much for him to bear.

The cot under the portia tree lay bare. He walked towards the door. A large iron lock hung on the latch. For a minute, he thought she had just hung the lock outside and latched the door from the inside. So he tried pushing the latch. It was chain-locked on the outside. All his intoxication wore off. He tried pushing the lock around. Was she teasing him? But why play with him at this time of the night and that too at his father-in-law's place? He leaned against the door and looked across the front yard. The bullocks were not there. Nor was the cart.

His lips murmured, 'She has cheated you, she has cheated you.'

He banged his head against the door. His topknot came undone and rolled down to his nape.

'You whore!' he shouted. 'Have you really gone? Have you gone despite my saying no?' Only the dog echoed his shout in a single bark. The hens that had climbed the portia tree rustled their feathers and marked their presence. 'All of you have gotten together and cheated me,' he cried.

His sobbing stopped gradually.

Suddenly, he got up like a man possessed. He opened the full bottle of arrack in his hand and drank it down in one gulp. He didn't stop for air even once. Holding the bottle in his hand, he started walking. His hair, now loosened completely, lashed like a whip across his back. He wobbled along slowly all the way back to his home.

When he reached his barnyard at dawn, his dog came running to him and showed him its affection by curling its body and getting between his feet. But he kicked it off. It screamed in pain and ran away. Under the portia tree, the cattle were munching on fodder. He sat on the rock under the tree. He drank some more of the arrack. When he yelled, 'You whore! You have cheated me!' he was breathless. 'You will not be happy. You have cheated me, you whore . . .'

He slid down to the ground. The rope running from the corn stacks pressed against his back. He looked above. The branches of the portia tree had spread themselves across the sky.

a note on the type

Bembo is one of the most comfortable and competent typefaces for extended texts. It exhibits a classic beauty: elegant without being fussy, and neither too condensed nor too expanded. Named after Pietro Bembo—a sixteenth-century Italian scholar, poet and cardinal—this serif typeface was first cut in 1495 by Francesco Griffo, a Venetian goldsmith who had become a punchcutter. Other well-known serif typefaces like Garamond and Times Roman exhibit characteristics that can be traced back to Bembo. This typeface was revived in 1929 by the superlative typographical talents of Stanley Morison, who successfully adapted the font to the machine requirements of the day. Morison's efforts have ensured that the Bembo font family lives on, the calligraphic style of its distinctive serifs imparting a warm human feel.

PYRE

'Murugan is the most accomplished of his generation of Tamil writers' *Caravan*

Saroja and Kumaresan are in love. After a hasty wedding, they arrive in Kumaresan's village, harbouring the dangerous secret that their marriage is an inter-caste one, likely to anger the villagers should they learn of it. Kumaresan is confident that all will be well. He naively believes that after the initial round of curious questions, the inquiries will die down and the couple will be left alone. But nothing is further from the truth. The villagers strongly suspect that Saroja must belong to a different caste. It is only a matter of time before their suspicions harden into certainty and, outraged, they set about exacting their revenge.

With spare, powerful prose, Murugan masterfully conjures a terrifying vision of intolerance in this devastating tale of innocent young love pitted against chilling savagery.

'Perumal Murugan's voice is distinct . . . [His] characters, dialogues and locales are unerringly drawn and intensely evocative . . . A superb writer' *Indian Express*

'[A] great literary chronicler . . . Murugan is at the height of his creative powers' *The Hindu*